SEALS

SOUL GUARDIANS BOOK 8

KIM RICHARDSON

Seals, Soul Guardians Book 8

Copyright © 2015 by Kim Richardson

Book cover by Damonza

www.kimrichardsonbooks.com

ISBN-13:978-1985247000

ISBN-10:1985247003

FABLEPRINT

BOOKS BY KIM RICHARDSON

SOUL GUARDIANS SERIES

Marked

Elemental

Horizon

Netherworld

Seirs

Mortal

Reapers

Seals

MYSTICS SERIES

The Seventh Sense

The Alpha Nation

The Nexus

DIVIDED REALMS

Steel Maiden

Witch Queen

Blood Magic

THE HORIZON CHRONICLES

The Soul Thief

The Helm of Darkness

The City of Flame and Shadow

The Lord of Darkness

To Kara, David, Jenny and Peter.
You guys are awesome.

SEALS

SOUL GUARDIANS BOOK 8

KIM RICHARDSON

1

CHAPTER 1
FLIGHT

Horizon was mad.

The supernatural world that Kara had grown to love and respect had gone off the deep end. Making deals with the Netherworld was like asking the wolf *not* to eat the scrumptious little rabbit. It was a contradiction. It didn't make sense. Horizon and the Netherworld had been at war with each other since the beginning of time. It was the ongoing ancient battle between good and evil, light and darkness. And now the light was letting the darkness in. It was preposterous, infuriating, and yet it *was* happening.

When Kara had first heard the news, she had been confused and shocked. But her confusion soon boiled into an uncontrollable, white-hot anger. The only way she would make it through the upcoming meeting without losing her temper and cutting a few higher demons would be to get out. Get out and fly.

Kara kicked off hard and let the wind cool her hot temper. She soared high above the outskirts of Green Bay, Wisconsin and practiced maneuvering with her newly formed wings until flying seemed second nature, anything to keep her mind off the ridiculous notion of making a deal with the devils. She stroked with her wings, again and again, until the city had disappeared beneath her, and she was alone in the sky.

She aimed for the clouds. And like a runner in thick fog, she could feel the vapor on her face as she flew through them. Like a great eagle, she glided above the clouds that hid her from mortal eyes and relaxed for the first time since the archangels Metatron and Ariel had told her about their arrangement with the higher demons.

She knew it was stupid and reckless to be out in full view for all mortal eyes to see, but she didn't care. Why should she care what the legion thought anyway? She wasn't the one siding with the enemy—*they* were. Besides, it was nearly dark out, and she didn't remember reading any rules about not being allowed to *fly* above the mortal world. Her wings were too new, and too unusual, for any decrees to have been written just yet.

And she was going to take advantage of it.

Her mind was in hyper-drive. She was so angry she wanted to scream. She had to focus elsewhere, and she concentrated on flying.

Flight was a constant learning curve. She wasn't born with wings, and there was no one to teach her, no petty officer to show her the ropes. She was on her own. She needed to practice as much as she could. It required a lot of effort just to support her weight at such a high altitude, and it would take many hours of flying to fly efficiently, let alone to defend herself and to attack.

However, right now she needed to clear her head. She had to forget this new pact with the Netherworld because she was losing her concentration. And it took loads of concentration not to plummet to the ground below.

And yet, as hard as she tried, the events of the recent meeting kept crawling back into her head. Kara gritted her teeth. The way the higher demons had sneered at her like they had won some secret victory enraged her. She couldn't shake off the feeling that somehow the demons had their own secret agenda. In fact, she was prepared to bet her angel life that they were using the archfiend's escape as a means of some evil plan of their own. They were demons after all, human-soul-eating monsters. They couldn't be trusted. They were up to something, and she was going to find out what.

As she banked softly to the left, she marveled at the sight of the city lights that blinked at her through holes in the clouds. She loved it up here and wished she could stay forever. She felt free. Free of responsibilities. Free from the changes that threatened her mind and body.

Kara didn't know how long she'd been flying when a throbbing pain suddenly erupted in her head and took over her body. Like a sudden wave of sickness, a cold sweat formed on her back and forehead and a chill shuddered through her.

She knew she couldn't stay up for much longer. A pulsing ache surged through her wings, and they faltered.

She wasn't sure how high she had flown, maybe six thousand feet, but the one thing she did know for sure was that if she fell now, her mortal suit wouldn't be able to withstand the impact. She would be no use to anyone as an exploded M-suit mess. As the throbbing increased, Kara tucked her wings in, banked a one-hundred-and-eighty-degree turn, and began her descent.

Falling was a pretty cool sensation. Ignoring the pain in her head and body, Kara smiled as she dive-bombed to the surface. The wind whistled in her ears. The air flapped at her face and clothes, and her hair spilled madly behind her. She grinned wildly.

She recognized the barn, and she raised her head and angled her body upward, spreading out her wings to slow her descent. She could see David and Ashley's smiling faces looking up at her. They may have been expecting some grand, graceful landing, but she hadn't *mastered* the art of landing yet, and she was going too fast.

She was going to crash.

Kara cursed. She wished they hadn't been there to see her make a fool of herself, especially David. She thrust her body backward in a desperate attempt to slow down. She swung her wings in a circular motion, back and forth, like giant hands clapping. She stuck out her legs in front of her like the ducks did when they landed in the pond at her grandma's cottage. But there was no pond here to slow her descent. The impenetrable ground looked more and more like a giant concrete runway than a soft farm field.

David ran toward her, arms stretched out like he wanted to catch her.

"Get out of the way!" yelled Kara. She waved her hands frantically in a desperate attempt to make him move away, but it only made him run faster toward her.

"What are you doing? I can't stop! Get out of the way—"

Kara rammed into David.

The force of the impact propelled them both into the air, and they skidded to a stop in a field of tall golden grass. She landed on top of him. With her wings folded behind her, Kara looked down into his blue eyes, and for a moment she forgot all about her wings, the higher demons, and the archfiends. There was only her and David in a farmer's meadow.

David pulled her closer, and his mouth twitched in a mischievous grin.

"I saved you, my darling butterfly."

Kara spit the grass from her mouth.

"You're delusional."

She tried to ignore how comfortable she felt with his arms around her.

"You didn't *save* me. I *crashed* into you, but I did try to warn you. Didn't you hear me?"

David's smile widened.

"You can crash into me any time, if it means I can hold you like this." He tightened his hold around her.

His eyes mesmerized her. He pulled her in closer to him, his lips dangerously near…

"Where is everyone?" Kara turned away from David's scrumptious lips before she did something stupid—like kiss him.

"Is the meeting over? I didn't realize I'd been gone that long. It didn't *feel* long. I guess I lost track of time."

"I'll give you the answer... *if* ... you give me a kiss."

Kara whirled around. "David, don't be stupid. I'm serious."

She tried to pull herself off of him, only too aware that Ashley was probably somewhere near, watching them with a scowl on her face. She wasn't sure how she'd feel about Ashley witnessing this. But she couldn't break away from his embrace, or maybe she just didn't want to.

"Come on, David, let me go. Wasn't Ashley with you?"

"Give me a kiss," said David again, "and I'll let you go. I swear it. Angel's honor." He puckered his lips.

Kara snorted. "*Angel's honor?* Are you kidding me? When did you ever have angel's honor?"

"Kiss me," David repeated, "and I'll tell you everything you want to know."

As much as this offer was tempting, Kara tried to pull away from him again, but her smile betrayed her.

"I swear, if you don't let me go this instant—"

David leaned in and kissed her. It was brief, but she felt its electricity from the tip of her wings to her toes. She missed his kisses. She wanted more. Much more.

Kara stared at his eyes and leaned in—

Someone cleared their throat.

David's grip loosened, and Kara jumped as far away from David as she could.

"I knew the rumors were true about you guys," laughed Ashley softly. She raised her hands when she saw the look of panic on Kara's face.

"Don't worry, your secret is safe with me. I wouldn't dream of telling anyone what I *saw*. And I saw *plenty*."

Kara was utterly mortified that Ashley had seen her private moment with David. Her angel life was already an open book for the entire legion to read. She wanted to keep some of it private.

Her wings ruffled in annoyance as she put more distance between herself and David. She tried her best to look natural, as natural as a winged creature could be.

"I hate to *interrupt* you," said Ashley, "but Ariel asked me and David to get you, Kara. I wasn't expecting he'd take it *literally*."

Kara wanted to tell Ashley that she hadn't interrupted anything, but she lost her voice when she looked back at David. He looked as if he had been rejected, like she was *ashamed* of him. Kara wanted to reach out to him, but the moment had passed

"We're all ordered to report back to Horizon for further instruction," said Ashley. She looked uneasily at David.

"I don't know about you guys, but this whole thing feels really rotten. I have to trust that the legion knows what they're doing. But I just don't know. I heard Ariel mention something to Metatron about teaming up with demons, but maybe I'm wrong."

Ashley shook her head, not wanting to believe that what she had heard might be true.

9

Kara glanced over at the barn uneasily.

"No, I'm sure you're right about what you heard. I wouldn't put anything passed Metatron, however disturbing it might sound."

She shuddered inwardly at her own mention of Metatron and turned her attention back to Ashley. "Has everyone left?"

Ashley nodded. "Yes. We're the last."

Kara looked up into the deep, navy sky. The memory of the archfiends soaring into the sky was still fresh in her mind, and she felt the panic that they brought with them again.

A war was brewing. It was inevitable. The threat was as real and as tangible as she was. She felt it in her soul. Could the legion defeat their archenemies? She didn't want to admit it to herself, but she was frightened at the hopelessness of their situation, frightened that they would lose this battle. She had never felt like this before. It was terrifying. She was losing hope.

"Things are going to be different now, with this new *arrangement*."

Kara did her best to try and hide her anxiety. "We have to prepare ourselves."

"I know," said Ashley. "It's not going to be easy. But what choice do we have?"

"We always have a choice," said Kara.

Ashley shook her head. "Not this time. Come on. Ariel's waiting for us. Let's get out of here and go home."

She made her way toward the small creek behind the barn.

Home. Kara felt disconnected. Even though she was still horribly angry with the legion, Horizon was *still* her home. She had to protect it from the archfiends. It was time to go back. She needed to check on her friends.

Jenny and Peter were still healing. The last time she had seen them, they were both in critical condition. She had saved them, but just barely. Now she missed their smiling faces. She missed the usual demon-killing routine. She needed normalcy.

Before Kara turned to follow Ashley, she reached out to David.

"David, I'm sorry—"

He brushed past her with his eyes on the ground and didn't even look at her.

Kara stood there for a moment, gathering herself, as she watched him walk away. What had she done that was so terrible? But even as she asked herself, she knew. She had hurt David more than she had realized when she had dismissed his affections in front of Ashley.

She watched the back of his head, the sway in his shoulders as he walked away, and still she couldn't move. It was like someone had punched her in the gut.

David arrived at the creek just behind Ashley. He didn't turn around. He just jumped into the creek and disappeared.

As Kara stood in her desolation, she felt a presence behind her, something foul, something *dead*.

She spun around and held her soul blade to the throat of a sneering higher demon.

The demon's grin widened so much that he looked like a ventriloquist's puppet.

"Aren't we a little bit jumpy, *fiend*-angel? We're supposed to be on the same team now. Remember? Why don't you put that blade away so we can have a nice little chat?"

Kara narrowed her eyes and pushed the blade harder into the demon's neck.

"I'll never be on *your* team, demon. I don't care what the legion says. I've always been a bit of a rebel, and I usually do things *my* way. Besides, I don't think killing just one demon will ruin the legion's plans. It's not like you'll be missed. Give me a reason why I shouldn't kill you now?"

"Because you'd be breaking the new treaty we have with the legion, and you'd be in a lot of trouble, little angel," laughed the higher demon.

"If you want to beat the archfiends…" the higher demon paused, licked its lips with a gray tongue and then added, "you *need* us. The archfiends will destroy all of us if they can, but *together* we stand a fighting chance. We can beat them."

Kara couldn't bring herself to admit the demon might be right. "I know you're up to something with this deal with Horizon, and I'm going to find out what it is."

"You're wrong…but then again you're the one with the blade."

Kara had never been so close to a higher demon for so long without killing it. The demon smelled of bile and rotten flesh, and it took an enormous amount of will power not to send it back to the Netherworld. She gritted her teeth.

"Why were you were sneaking behind me, *demon*?"

"I was not."

"Liar," spat Kara. A trickle of black blood seeped down the tip of her blade.

"All you demons are liars. It's part of what you are—deceivers and tricksters. There's nothing honest about demons. You might have fooled Ariel and the other archangels, but I'm not buying this sham. This treaty's a joke. *You* know it, and *I* know it."

A rasping laugh erupted from the demon's throat. "You angels are so suspicious, you especially. I meant no offense. I was just *curious* about you, that is all."

There was something odd with the way the demon said *curious*, almost as though it hinted that it knew something about her, about what was happening to her ... about her wings. But how could that be?

"We wanted a closer look at your new *wings*," said a second voice from behind her, as though it had been reading her mind.

Kara turned quickly and saw two more higher demons.

Between them was a man. He looked like a regular thirty-year-old businessman in an expensive black suit. He had neatly trimmed dark hair and a sly smile on his handsome face. He looked like he was ready to charm his way into some sort of cunning deal. But his black eyes and pale skin gave him away. Although he looked like a model, he still smelled like the dead. He was a demon. He carried himself like a proud peacock, and Kara suspected she was looking at a demon lord or some kind of boss from the Netherworld. Typical. She narrowed her eyes. She wanted to kill him too.

"They are..."

The man-demon paused as he took a moment to inspect her wings thoroughly, moving his black eyes over every inch of her, "…remarkable."

"I know."

Kara shoved her captive higher demon to the ground and resisted the urge to kick it. The demon smiled at her viciously and then stood amongst its brethren. Their hollow black eyes and their identical faces were warped and twisted into unnaturally large sneers. These higher demons, clones from the abyss, always freaked her out.

She sensed that they were hiding something, like they knew some sort of secret about her that they weren't about to share. She was really starting to get annoyed.

"If you don't stop staring at me like that, I'm going to start chopping off heads."

"So you're the infamous Kara Nightingale," said the man. He stood too close, and his black eyes rolled over her body once more.

"My, my. You're not at all what I expected."

Kara grimaced at his foul breath and shuddered at his nearness, but she wouldn't move. Showing this demon any kind of weakness by stepping back would be a victory for him. She wouldn't give him the satisfaction. So instead, she squared her shoulders and raised her chin. "Yeah? And why's that?"

He raised his brows. "I imagined you…taller. But, you're still very…exquisite."

The frown on Kara's face deepened. "And you are?"

"Salthazar," said the demon pompously. His voice was oily and treacherous. It was the voice of a madman.

Kara twirled her blade in her hand, inches from Salthazar's suit.

"You say that like it's supposed to mean something to me." She forced a laugh. "Never heard of you."

Salthazar lost his smile for a second, but when it returned, and to Kara's surprise, his teeth were sparkling white.

"No matter, you will hear of me soon enough. But to help enlighten you—I'm your late father's successor."

Kara flinched as though Salthazar had slapped her across the face. With all that was happening to her, and with the archfiends' escape, the last thing on her mind was her father, the demon lord that *she* had killed.

"Yes," continued Salthazar.

He clearly enjoyed the distress on Kara's face.

"We all know what you did to your own precious daddy. You were the talk of the Netherworld for a long time, the angel that destroyed the powerful Asmodeus. He was the strongest and greatest of our kind, and yet *you...*" his black eyes sparkled, "...destroyed him. How did you do it?"

A smile tugged at the corners of her lips. "It just happened."

"Nothing ever *just* happens. There is always an explanation. Was it cleverness? Wit? Strength? Or just dumb luck? I guess we'll never really know how you managed to vanquish the most powerful demon lord of our time."

Kara let out a growl of annoyance. "Guess not."

Salthazar watched her for a moment. "Rumors spread of your elemental power. Yes. I know of it. It sparked lots of interest amongst our kind—to be able to control such wild and fierce energy. It is a power that demons have long desired to manipulate ourselves. But we never succeeded. Your father tried and failed. It must take a great deal of self-control, not to let it control you. But I guess things have changed now. I know that you don't possess it anymore."

Kara did her best to hide her annoyance and bitterness. Her elemental power was gone, and she felt miserable. It had left a hole in her, and she wanted it back.

The demon lord shook his head. "You lost an incredible gift, there's no denying that…only to be replaced by wings? Don't you think it's strange that these things keep happening to you, Kara Nightingale of the legion of angels? Yes…tell me, why is that?"

"It's a mystery."

Kara gripped the handle of her dagger. Her nails cut into her palm. She tried to ignore the surge and crash of bitter emotions that had awoken within her. Truth be told, she wished she knew the answer, too. But she didn't. She didn't know why these horrible things kept happening to her, the elemental power…the wings…it was like a dark force kept throwing obstacles at her, challenging her, keeping her from becoming the guardian she was supposed to become, keeping her from attaining her full potential.

Salthazar let out a cold laugh. "Well, whatever. I think I should be thanking you, really. Without you, without what you did, I wouldn't be here. So thank you for clearing a path for me."

He paused. "I've always wondered why *you* didn't take his place."

Kara frowned, but she couldn't find her voice.

"You could have, you know," continued the demon. "It was rightfully yours. You could have taken your father's place in the Netherworld. To rule the demons as their queen."

"My job is to *kill* demons," said Kara. She trembled with rage and squeezed her soul blade. "That's what guardian angels do. We rid the earth of scum like you, and we protect the mortals. I would *never* side with you, with demons. I would rather die a thousand true deaths than join the Netherworld."

Salthazar laughed harder. "So very dramatic, but then again all you angels are such *dramatic* creatures. But you..." he faltered, "but you're *different*, aren't you, Kara? You've never been just a *regular* angel. You're different. You always have been, and never more so than now."

His eyes moved to her wings, and Kara squeezed them together in an unsuccessful attempt to hide them behind her back.

The demon raised his eyebrows and waved his hands in a dismissal.

"Never mind. Well then, that's settled."

He raised his voice. "I'm Lord Salthazar, ruler of the Netherworld. I'm taking over where Asmodeus left off."

"What do you want?" growled Kara, unable to control the hatred and anger that boiled inside her. She wanted to cut that pretty smile off Salthazar's face.

The demon lord smiled at Kara's sudden rage. He was enjoying seeing her struggle internally. He wanted to push her buttons. He was testing her.

He regarded her silently for a moment and then said, "Just wanted a look. I wanted to see who this famous Kara Nightingale was, the little girl who killed the powerful Asmodeus, the one who's been brewing up such trouble in my world. I wanted to see what the fuss was all about."

His black eyes widened. "But most of all, I wanted to see your wings. I wanted to see them in all their *glory* myself."

Kara felt the eyes of all the higher demons on her. Their gray, identical faces were frozen like ugly life-size demonic dolls. Their black eyes glimmered with evil. How could Horizon make a deal with these treacherous, vile creatures?

She glowered. "Well, you've seen them, so get lost."

She waved her blade menacingly at the demon's face, knowing all too well that demon lords were powerful and that her puny blade probably wouldn't do much damage.

Salthazar laughed playfully as though Kara had said something very funny. "Of course."

His black eyes rolled over her body once more, and she resisted the urge to shiver under his creepy, oily stare.

"See you soon, *butterfly*," he said and turned on his heel.

"Not if I can help it."

Kara hated the fact that only moments ago David had called her that, too. But now, hearing it from the lips of the demon lord made her feel dirty somehow.

Kara watched the demons leave. Butterflies were beautiful and fragile, while Kara was nothing of the sort. She wasn't weak, and she would prove it.

But first she'd have to apologize to David.

Just as she turned to leave, a choking, mind-searing pain burst from her chest and extended to her fingertips and to her wings. White lights exploded from behind her eyes like a giant migraine, like someone beating her head with a sledgehammer. Her ears popped, and she could scarcely hear her own screams. She was on fire, burning from the inside out. She closed her eyes. She could feel her body swell. She was changing into something else.

Kara dropped her blade and crumbled to her knees. The weight of her wings was like a backpack full of bricks. It pinned her to the ground and paralyzed her. She could feel the infection coursing through her. She gritted her teeth as another spasm of pain hit her. What was happening to her? Fear replaced her pain. She was sick with trembling and felt a madness infecting her mind. Darkness. Evil...

She struggled desperately to cling to her sanity—to herself. But it was no use. Fighting it was useless. The darkness was now part of her, like a piece of her soul. She couldn't stop it. It consumed her.

And then the pain subsided, and she could move again. But she was different. She could sense it.

With a trembling hand, she pulled up her sleeve and held back a scream.

Intricate designs of large black veins throbbed in her arm from her wrist to her elbow, foul and monstrous.

She was changing, and not into a beautiful butterfly. She was becoming an abominable and evil monster.

CHAPTER 2

THE FOUR KNIGHTS

Three days had passed since the archfiends had escaped from their eternal prisons. Dark clouds had formed over the entire mortal world, and the sun hadn't shone in three days.

Kara stood in what was left of Mr. Patterson's bookstore. It wasn't much. It had four walls and a roof, and it looked like it'd been hit by a tornado. With the help of Jenny, Peter, Ashley and David, she had done her best to rebuild his shop with old planks of wood and drywall that hadn't been destroyed by the imps. They had created a haphazard building with a crooked roof, boarded up windows, mismatched exterior siding, and trickling wet gray paint that oozed from the boarded windows. The bookstore looked like it was crying.

While the rest of the legion were making important and secretive plans with the servants and Lords of the Netherworld,

Kara and her friends had been charged with rebuilding one of the safe houses. They had chosen Jim's Old Bookstore, partly because it was one of the key safe houses, but mostly because they felt a close connection to the place.

It pained Kara to see the look on Mr. Patterson's face as he picked up the remains of his beloved collections of books, magazines, and other memorabilia. He looked like he'd just lost a member of his family. His books were a part of him. Even though they had rebuilt his store—Kara knew it would never be the same.

Just like her. Too much had happened. Too much had been damaged and couldn't be fixed. She couldn't be fixed.

That's exactly how Kara felt about herself. She was damaged goods. No one could stop the mutation from happening. The black veins continued to spread, and darkness coursed through her mind. It was like developing some deadly disease. She was watching her body change. She barely recognized herself. All she could do was wait in pain for the mysterious transformation that preoccupied her to manifest itself completely. The lingering hope that she *could* fight the demon that dwelled inside and wanted to come out was fading away.

The white oracle mother had told her that she was, indeed, part archfiend, or something along those lines—a monster. She had *seen* that in her, and Kara had *seen* it, too.

The white oracle had showed her a world of fire—buildings burned and smoked as millions of dead mortals lay piled and splayed out on the streets of dead cities. She remembered the sound of people dying in battle. She remembered seeing Horizon burning

22

and devastated. But worst of all, the white oracle had shown her herself...or the black-hearted angel-killing monster that she was to become.

Kara wanted to scream at the injustice of it all. She had screamed in the sky many times before. Alone in the sky, her screams echoed like thunder.

The white oracle had said, *"Remember who you are, Kara. You can still change the future."*

Kara planned on doing just that. She was going to change the future. She just didn't know how, exactly, she was going to do it.

Kara focused on the bookstore. Although they had managed to salvage half the books, the store would never be the same. The cheery old bookstore with its knickknacks and smell of mothballs and burnt wood still looked abandoned. Even their hopeful attempts to find the bookstore's sign and lift everyone's gloomy spirits had failed miserably. There was no more sign. There was nothing but ash and crumpled chunks of plaster.

Mr. Patterson had lost the bounce in his step and the twinkle in his eyes. The escape of the archfiends weighed heavily on him, but Kara was sure most of his gloom was caused by the destruction of his shop and the loss of his cherished crystals.

Most of his crystals had been destroyed in the fight with the imps. And now, Mr. Patterson stood behind what was left of his counter, which was nothing more than a taped cardboard box with legs, and polished his last remaining crystal ball.

Kara wished she could do something to help him.

Suddenly, the old man's face slackened and he looked as if he were far away, like he was in a trance. His blue eyes and skin blazed and turned a soft golden color. The crystal ball shimmered and glowed brighter. Its insides churned until it was glowing like a tiny brilliant star. She knew he was *seeing* or communicating with the legion. He would be *gone* for a while. Maybe it was better this way. It would keep him preoccupied with matters of the legion. He needed a break from the devastation that was his bookstore.

Kara sighed. Her thoughts returned to her own gloom, and her eyes settled on David.

During the days of rebuilding, David still hadn't uttered a word to Kara. He didn't much look at her either, and he ignored her many attempts to apologize. When they had returned to Horizon, Kara had joined David and Ashley as they had welcomed back Jenny and Peter from the Healing-Xpress. But David had ignored her completely. He was his usual friendly self with everyone except her, and that made everyone else uncomfortable, too. Jenny kept looking at Kara for an explanation. But she had no answers, nothing she wanted to admit yet, so all she could do was look down. She had made a real mess of things with David.

But she was determined to make it right.

Even now as he hammered the last nail into a supporting beam, David was a lot quieter than usual. His face was pinched, but it couldn't hide his handsome square jaw and his perfect cheekbones. When he finished nailing the beam, David tossed his hammer into a red toolbox and moved toward Peter, who was painting the back wall very badly.

24

Did David know she was watching him? If he did, he didn't show it. He continued to avoid her gaze.

Kara could feel Jenny's eyes on her while she and Ashley organized some of the books on the rescued bookshelves. But Kara couldn't look at her. She didn't want to see the pity in her eyes.

"Kara?" she heard Jenny's voice. "Since when do you wear gloves?"

Kara braced herself as everyone, even David, turned to look at her hands. She could feel their eyes like laser beams piercing through her black leather gloves. If she had been a mortal girl, her face would have been beet red. Thank goodness she wasn't.

Kara stared at her hands. Her chest tightened. She hadn't told anyone about the mysterious black marks on her arms. The markings had started to spread to her legs as well. She had panicked and hid her hands with a pair of leather gloves she had found back in the lockers at the Counter Demon Division.

It was a foolish way to try and pretend the *change* wasn't happening. She felt it in her body, felt it in her soul. There was no denying it anymore—she was changing. First she had sprouted wings, then ugly black veins on her arms and legs, and then...

Kara looked up at Jenny and forced a smile. "Thought these black gloves would look cool with my new wings. You know, thought I'd make it a *look* or something."

Jenny's bright green eyes sparkled in delight.

"Yeah, totally. You look amazing. Maybe we could find you a complete leather outfit? That would be *killer*. You'd look so badass in leather."

The spark faded in Jenny's eyes for a moment.

"I wish I had wings. Then we could fly together and beat those stupid archfiends."

Jenny's camaraderie only made Kara feel worse about lying to everyone, especially to David.

Kara kept her eyes on Jenny. "Let's start with just the gloves. I'm not sure how flexible a leather jumpsuit would be."

"It is time!" announced Mr. Patterson.

He made his way to the center of the bookstore, and Kara could see that his bare feet were dangerously close to sharp wood splinters. His eyes gleamed their natural blue again, and he held his crystal close to his chest, like he was protecting it, as though he feared it would suddenly burst.

As they gathered around the old man, Kara's eyes automatically went to David. She expected him to say something sarcastic or make a joke, as he always did. But his lips were tight, and his eyes never left Mr. Patterson. It was like she wasn't even there, like she didn't exist to him, not anymore.

David's indifference felt a lot worse than her stupid mutation.

"It is as I feared," said the old man.

He looked like he'd aged a few centuries during the past three days. His eyes were bruised with deep circles.

"What is?" said Kara as she found her voice. She tensed. Did David just look at her?

Mr. Patterson closed his eyes. "The end of days."

Kara and Jenny exchanged worried looks.

"I've just received vital information about what is to come," continued Mr. Patterson.

He opened his eyes. "I wished...I prayed to the souls that I might be wrong...but as usual, I was not."

"The end of days," repeated Ashley solemnly, and as she shook her head, her long blond ponytail brushed across her shoulders. "You mean the end of the world? Because of the archfiends? Because they escaped?"

Mr. Patterson nodded. "The apocalypse. It has already begun. The archfiends have cast a shadow over the sun. You have already seen it."

"This is bad," said Jenny as she crossed her arms.

"It gets worse," said Mr. Patterson. "Without the sun, the earth will freeze over. Without the sun, plants will no longer be able to inhale carbon dioxide and exhale the life-sustaining oxygen that mortals and all living things need. By the end of this week, the average surface temperature will be below the freezing point. The planet's ocean surfaces will freeze over. Temperatures have already started to drop. Within a year or so most of the human population will die. Life on Earth cannot survive without the sun. The planet will die. The archfiends want death."

Peter cursed and then raised his brows at everyone's shocked expression.

"This is serious stuff. My uncle owns a farm, that's how he supports his family."

"His farm will not last." The old man shook his head. "If we don't stop their *infection*, it will ultimately destroy *all* the worlds.

27

They will start with this one and then move on to the others. First, the archfiends will cloak mortal world in darkness, and then they will unleash their…"

He faltered. His lips moved but no sound escaped his mouth.

Kara leaned forward. "Their what?"

Mr. Patterson lowered his voice. "Their four *knights*."

A strange tingling spread over Kara's body. "Their *four knights*?"

"SHHH!"

Mr. Patterson jumped on the spot. His eyes widened, and he looked over his shoulder, as if he were expecting these knights to suddenly appear. He clasped his crystal closer to his chest like a safety blanket. "Do not speak their name so loudly."

"Okay, sorry." Kara raised her gloved hands in apology.

She caught David's eye, and for a moment she couldn't speak. His face was unreadable, but he was *looking* at her. There was eye contact, and that was definitely a huge improvement. She tried not to show her relief in her face or in her voice.

"So what are they, these creatures? The ones we shouldn't name?" she asked and reluctantly moved her eyes away from David, feeling his eyes still on her.

Mr. Patterson lowered his voice again. "The *four knights* of the apocalypse."

The tingling rolled up Kara's back and spread to her fingers.

"Why do I get the feeling this is really, really bad." Peter stared at a spot on his right arm where the imps had dug out the key to unlock their master's prison. He looked frightened, and Kara felt sorry for him.

"Because it probably is." David stood with his hands in his pockets. His eyes looked wild.

"Expect the worse, man, and you won't be disappointed. Trust me. It's been working for me lately." He glanced at Kara, and she felt a stabbing pain in her chest.

Mr. Patterson coughed lightly and waited to get everyone's attention before continuing.

"When the archfiends broke out of their prison, it began a series of events that will ultimately culminate in war—war of the worlds. The darkness will bring the four..."

He paused and added with a whisper, "*Knights* of the apocalypse."

Kara flinched. The tingling inside her worsened.

"Each knight possesses unique abilities that correspond to their apocalyptic roles."

Kara's tingling started to burn inside her. Something was definitely wrong, but she kept a straight face.

"The first one is War," explained Mr. Patterson. "This knight can alter human perception and make people see enemies when there are none. It creates hatred and mistrust and ultimately creates wars between nations. The second knight is Famine. This creature begins by destroying all the earth's natural resources, then it will turn on mortals themselves and drive their hungers and addictions for the food and resources it has destroyed. The third knight is Pestilence. This horrible wraith creates and manipulates deadly human diseases until the entire world is plagued with sickness."

Kara swayed slightly and braced herself against her increasing pain.

Mr. Patterson paused, as though he were gathering up the courage to continue.

"The last and most deadly of all the knights is the one called *Death*—"

Kara cried out in agony.

She doubled over and clasped her chest as searing, white-hot pain coursed through her insides.

CHAPTER 3

THE FOUR RINGS

Kara could feel the black veins like tiny, sharp knives inside her. They twisted and sliced as they made their way up her legs and surrounded her torso. She convulsed as another tidal wave of pain rolled inside her. She screamed a silent scream, aware that everyone was watching her turn into a monster.

Her embarrassment and desperation to make whatever was happening to her stop seemed to force the pain to subside, but she knew it wouldn't last for very long.

"Kara? What is it?"

Kara blinked the spots away from her eyes. David was right beside her, and she felt his hands holding her up. She wanted to smile, but she couldn't feel her face.

"Come, come over here and sit down." He cradled her, careful not to pull on her wings as he balanced her weight. Not that she had the strength to refuse. Her delight at his sudden change of heart made the pain worth it. At least now he was speaking to her.

He led her to a small wooden chair that hadn't been destroyed by the imps and sat her down. Her wings hung heavily over the sides of the chair like thick drapes. They were more of a burden than she cared to admit. David clasped her gloved hand in his and knelt beside her.

"Kara. What the heck is happening to you? What was that?"

Kara still held her stomach with her left arm.

"Cramps from the wings," she lied as she waited for the tremors of pain to lessen.

"I think I've been overdoing it with my hours of flying practice. I stayed up there for too long, and I've over exerted myself. I'm still trying to get used to these new wings. I'll be fine in a minute. It's really not that big a deal."

David didn't look convinced, but he didn't press her.

He continued to hold her hand and said, "I'm sorry for being such an idiot before. I haven't been myself lately."

"I know," said Kara. Her eyes searched into his, and she gave him the tiniest of smiles.

And from the way his look softened, she knew that it was all she'd ever needed to say. It was a silent apology that they both offered and accepted.

Mr. Patterson frowned. "Are you sure you're feeling all right? You gave us all quite a fright."

He leaned forward. "You say that your wings caused this outburst?"

Kara sank back into the chair, her face neutral as the old man inspected her. "It's really no big deal, just cramps from over doing it with my wings. I'm fine, really. It's passed."

"Well, it didn't *look* fine," said Mr. Patterson. "You looked like you were in a great deal of pain, as though *something* was hurting you."

He watched her for a moment. "Is there something you want to tell me?"

Kara hated how Mr. Patterson always seemed to be able to read her mind. Maybe oracles had mind reading powers. Did he know about the veins? Did all her friends know how much she was still changing.

Their terrified looks showed that they were all thinking the same thing. *How long until she changes completely?* How long until she becomes an angel-killing monster.

She looked at her friends. "I'm sorry I made everyone jump. It's nothing. I promise."

Desperate to change the subject and to keep David next to her she asked, "So, tell us about the last knight…the one you called *Death*. Why is he the worst of the four?"

"Death," repeated Mr. Patterson, "has control over all life: animal, human, angel, and even death itself."

An icy shiver rippled through Kara's body. She did not want to come face to face with this knight. But something inside her told her otherwise. Somehow she knew she would *have* to face this demon, just like she would have to come to terms with her own.

Mr. Patterson flicked a spec of lint off his crystal ball.

"Now, listen carefully, all of you. We kept the archfiends confined with additional layers of protection. Four seals were created. These seals derive their strength from this mortal world and protect against the archfiends' power. They are not physical things like this crystal here. Think of them as invisible bonds or locks that can only be broken if the mortal world from which the seals draw their power is destroyed. The energy of life itself and everything mortal that is bound to this earth is what keeps the seals strong. Destroy the earth, and the seals are broken."

He paused for a moment and then continued, "Over the years, we've heard rumors that the archfiends had figured out a way to break the seals. We dismissed these rumors. But we were wrong."

The old man was silent for a moment, his eyes cold and hard. "Even in their confinement, the archfiends were still more powerful than we believed. Over time they created the knights to be their champions. The knights are the keys that will enable the archfiends to escape their confinement."

"So what's the link between these knights and the seals?" asked Kara.

Mr. Patterson fixed her with a stare. "We believe the knights were somehow created from the seals themselves, or they possess some essence derived from the seals. In any case it appears that they can *break* the seals. Four knights for four seals, and as each knight completes his carnage upon the mortal world, the seals will break and the locks on the archfiend prisons will fail."

Kara shifted in her seat. "But I thought the archfiends were already *out* of their dungeon."

"They are, yes," said Mr. Patterson. "But in order for the archfiends to *remain* here indefinitely and to rule the worlds, the four knights must *break* their seals to destroy the prison. When the last seal is broken, lightning, earthquakes, hail, fire, mass extinction, poisoned waters, and monsters will plague the earth. The real carnage, the real apocalypse starts only when the four knights have broken the four seals."

"Perfect," said David. "Just what we need. I think I'd like to take my two weeks of vacation time now. I hear the beaches in Jamaica are to die for."

Mr. Patterson scowled at David. His fingers twitched around his crystal, and for a moment Kara thought he was about to smack David in the head with it.

"Does the legion know about this?" Peter stepped forward. Ever since he and Jenny had come back from the Healing-Xpress, Peter had looked and acted differently. He seemed older somehow, and there was a darkness in his eyes that wasn't there before. Kara could see new determination in him. He wanted payback for what had happened to him. It was both exciting and scary at the same time, like a loose cannon.

Mr. Patterson raised his brows. "They do."

"So what are they going to do about it?" said Peter with resentment in his voice, as though he blamed the legion for everything that had happened.

Mr. Patterson looked drained.

"The legion doesn't think the knights pose as big a threat as the archfiends. In fact, they are all connected."

35

He sighed.

"As we speak, the legion is forming combat strategies with demons from the Netherworld. They believe they'll have the upper hand in strength, with the help of the demons. And they will strike the archfiends soon."

Kara surveyed the old man's face. "But you *don't* think that's a good idea."

She knew him well enough to know when he was in silent disagreement, which was the case with her most of the time when she had worked for him at the bookstore.

The old man looked at her. His frown deepened and a great wave of sadness rolled over his face.

"I don't. I believe going after the archfiends will deliver a devastating blow upon us. The archfiends are too powerful. Even now, when they are not at their fullest strength, they are the most powerful creatures in all the worlds. They are an unstoppable, destructive force. The legion underestimates their power."

"I think..." he paused and shook his head. "No, I *know* the archfiends will be expecting our attack. They will slaughter us."

"Then you have to warn them," cried Jenny suddenly. "Ariel is going out there. Our friends will *die*."

She raised her voice even more. "You must tell her!"

"I have," said Mr. Patterson somberly. "We have, the oracles *and* the oracle mothers have told them many times. But the legion chose *not* to listen."

"So that's it?" Ashley shook her head and shrugged. "We just sit here and wait for the end of the world? We can't just do nothing. There's got to be another way."

Kara watched Mr. Patterson. "There's something else, isn't there? You've found out something, something that can help us. Tell us what it is. If there's a way to stop this, I want to know, and I don't care how crazy it sounds."

"Get ready for crazy," said David.

Mr. Patterson was silent for a moment, as though he was debating whether to let them in on his secret. Kara saw the smallest trace of a spark in his eyes.

"But all is not lost."

"You're speaking in riddles again, old man." David finally let go of Kara's hand and stood up. "If you've got something to say...if you have a plan in that big head of yours, by all means...we're listening."

Despite the seriousness of their end-of-the-world conversation, Mr. Patterson smiled. "I believe I have."

He looked at Kara and her friends for a moment and then added with more conviction, "I believe we *still* have a chance to win, to come out victorious...to save the worlds."

"Which is?" David crossed his arms over his chest, unconvinced, and glanced at Peter. But Peter looked hopeful and moved a little closer to hear the old man's plan.

Mr. Patterson patted a round bundle inside his jacket pocket.

"I've spoken to the oracles and the oracle mothers, and we've come up with a plan. We cannot destroy what is indestructible, but we can find a way to *confine* it."

Another wave of pain surged through Kara, and she fought hard keep her voice steady. "You mean to put them back into their cage?"

"Exactly."

"But…" Kara grimaced. The pain was like hot wax being poured on her wings. But then it subsided a little, and she was glad that the others had mistakenly read her scowl as intense determination instead of pain.

"The archfiends aren't stupid. I doubt they're going to fall again for whatever *trick* the legion used to lock them up in the first place."

"Exactly," said Mr. Patterson again.

His face brightened. "Which is why it's brilliant and why it's *going* to work. They won't be *expecting* us to try it again."

The five guardians all stared at the little man in stunned silence.

Mr. Patterson's eyes narrowed as he surveyed them all again. He looked a little offended that they didn't think his plan was a brilliant one.

David forced a laugh. "Told you it'd be crazy—no, it's insane. We can't succeed when the archfiends have seen the plan before."

"Not necessarily." Kara studied the oracle. "You must have something up your sleeve to go with your *brilliant* plan. Well?"

Mr. Patterson spoke feverishly. "To stop the apocalypse, we must stop the archfiends, and to do that…we must *seal* them back in their prison."

He paused and watched the confused expressions on the guardians' faces and decided to elaborate. "Theoretically, their cage is still there. It still exists. It was never destroyed but merely *opened.*"

Kara shifted excitedly in her chair, her pain forgotten. "So we can lock them back in. This is good, right? But can we actually *do* it?"

Her enthusiasm died as she looked at Peter.

"But how? The key was lost…they took it and have probably destroyed it by now."

Peter looked as if he were reliving the savage imp attack that had nearly cost him his angel life.

Mr. Patterson nodded and held up a finger. "Yes, the key to their cage was destroyed, but there *is* another way."

Glad to have their fullest attention now, he continued excitedly. "The archfiends' enclosure was originally secured by five different seals or five different locks if you will. The first seal was broken with the Keeper's key which unlocked the prison."

Everyone's eyes turned to Peter.

"But, as I said before, for the archfiends to regain their strength in our worlds, the other four seals *must* be broken. And since the four knights have the ability to break the remaining four seals, we believe if we can stop the knights, then the archfiends will be *forced back* into their abysmal prison."

Silence fell, and then Kara asked, "And why's that exactly?"

"The life-force that protects us is bound to the seals. If a knight fails to break his seal, part of the prison wall will rebuild itself. If all four of the knights fail, the archfiends will be forced back into their cage, and the seals *will* lock the cage forever."

Kara gripped the sides of her chair and straightened herself. "So we need to keep the knights from breaking the seals. We can win the war if we can actually *do* this."

"That is correct."

And then it hit her. If somehow she could get the archfiends back into their cage, then maybe the *infection* they had injected in her with would die, too. It made sense. If the archfiends' power was linked to the seals, then they needed to break the seals to complete her transformation. At last, Kara felt hopeful. She had found the way to reverse the curse. She felt like she'd been given a giant dose of antibiotics. She felt great. No, she felt amazing.

"Don't get too excited," said David.

He began to pace the room but then stopped and turned around to face the old man. "You said you *believe*. And you said it a few times. Why do I get the feeling that part of you isn't sure that your master plan is going to work?"

"Nothing in this life or the next is sure," said Mr. Patterson.

David raised his brows at Mr. Patterson, and then the little man said, "It's a working theory—"

"What?" Jenny let out an exasperated sigh. "We're supposed to risk our angel souls on a theory?"

Mr. Patterson's smile faded away completely. He looked put out. He had just given them their best chance, and they had spit it back in his face. Jenny's expression softened when she realized she'd upset him.

"Sorry Mr. P, but it's not good enough. I don't know if I'm willing to risk my angel life on a theory."

"It's the best thing we've got." Kara stood up.

Her pain was barely noticeable, if she didn't think about it too much. She fluttered her wings and stretched the stiffness out of them. She yanked up her gloves and made fists with her hands.

"We don't really have a choice. Just think about it for a minute. We already know that these creatures are even more powerful than the archangels. We know the legion had already tried and failed to destroy them. And I have a strong feeling that the archfiends are just as strong as they ever were, maybe more now that they have these knights. The legion won't be able to stop them, so our best chance is to follow Mr. Patterson's plan. We have to try."

She wasn't about to tell everyone that this plan might save her, too. She was determined to proceed, with or without them.

"So, how do we stop these knights? Where do we start?"

Mr. Patterson looked grim. "That, I do not know—"

"Fantastic," grumbled David. He kicked a chunk of drywall on the floor. "A great start to the master plan."

"All I know," said Mr. Patterson after he had glared at David and had gripped his crystal in one hand like a baseball, "is that these creatures will be more powerful than anything you've ever faced. We don't know even what they look like—"

"More good news," said David.

41

"They're probably riders of some sort, maybe riding on a beast."

The old man lowered his voice and turned to Kara. "This is where your wings will be most useful. Maybe they are a blessing in disguise."

"I seriously doubt that," said Kara, hiding her frustration. She knew Mr. Patterson was only trying to make her feel a little better. He cared about her, and that always brought her great comfort. But she also had the feeling that he knew more about her wings and her transformation than he was letting on.

"The best advice I can give you is to follow the trail of carnage, and you will find them."

Mr. Patterson paused and tapped his crystal ball thoughtfully. "How to defeat them is another great mystery, but take comfort in knowing that everything has a weakness. It's only a matter of finding what *that* is."

He gave Kara an encouraging smile. "Starting now, we have *four* days to stop the knights from completing their mission."

He turned and looked at David. "We *know* it will take seven days for the knights to break the seals. Unfortunately they have a three day start on us."

David growled. "So we've already lost three days. Super."

Kara's wings quivered with anticipation. She was restless to get started and did her best to hide her smile. The sooner they got rid of the knights, the sooner she'd be back to normal. At that moment she didn't care how all-powerful these supreme beings probably were, she only cared about ridding herself of her mutation.

Though she'd never admit it, Kara didn't really know what to expect when they faced the first knight. Her weapons training and fighting skills had made her an exceptional guardian. She knew this. But her body ached and hiding the throbbing pain in her wings was nearly impossible. They all thought her wings would be advantageous, but they didn't know how much she suffered. She had to keep up with the charade for everyone's sake. Whatever dangers lay ahead would decide the fate of them all, the fate of the worlds.

Their plan *was* going to work, because it *had* to.

"Four days left. One day for each knight. Sounds reasonable enough, and the day is just beginning," she said almost to herself, nodding. "Piece of cake, right?"

"If you say so." Ashley's expression was dark.

"Look," said Kara. "Just think of them as demons—only bigger and more powerful—but they're still malevolent creatures that have infected this world. And it's still our job, our mandate, to protect the mortal world with whatever it takes. And we're going to do what we do best. Hunt them down and destroy them. All of them."

She felt David's eyes on her but she ignored him.

"It's already been three days since their escape. How do we know if they haven't broken one of the seals already? And how will we know when they do?"

"Of course, we thought of that." Mr. Patterson held his crystal with one hand and rummaged inside his jacket pocket with the other. He pulled out four gold rings.

"The oracle mothers were able to forge these four rings from the same material that was used to create the Keeper's key. The materials are connected with the seals. They're bonded. If a seal is broken, one of the rings will disappear. And as you can see, no seal has been broken, not yet."

He held out his hand. "Come on, take one."

To Kara's surprise, David was the first to grab a ring and slip it on his finger. Then Jenny and Peter each grabbed a ring.

One ring left. But Kara couldn't move.

She suspected that she shouldn't take the last ring. What if it didn't work because of her transformation? The ring should go to an angel who wasn't tainted, an angel of pure essence. She pressed her hands into fists. Besides, she was wearing gloves. The ring wouldn't fit over them, and everyone would see the marks on her hands if she took them off. She couldn't risk it. Not yet.

She turned away from the ring momentarily and looked at Ashley.

"Take it," said Kara. She was surprised that the words had come out so easily, even though she felt a pang in her chest. "Take the ring."

Ashley shook her head. "No way. We all know it should be you, Kara. Besides, I'm new to your club, so I'm practically a rookie. But if you want the truth, I'd really rather not have that responsibility. Just being here with all of you is enough for me."

Kara knew Ashley still mourned the loss of her friends to the Reapers. Some part of her still blamed herself for their deaths, even though there was nothing she could have done to save them.

Joining with Kara's team had helped Ashley in her recovery, but she'd never truly recover. Not really.

"I wouldn't want to step on anyone's toes, especially yours." Ashley grinned with a sincere friendship that was loyal and would never break.

Kara wanted to smile, too, but she feared the repercussions of revealing too much too soon. Should she take the gloves off? No. It was too soon. She wasn't ready. They weren't ready. She wasn't ready to see the fear and disgust in David's eyes when he discovered the black veins on her hands and body.

"Go on, Kara." Mr. Patterson moved forward and offered her the last ring, like he had already decided it was going to be her.

"Ashley is right, it should be you. *You* should be the bearer of the last ring."

She *couldn't* take her gloves off, so she grabbed the last ring and examined it for a moment. It was heavier than any gold ring she'd ever handled, more like two rings in one. Then she put it in her pocket.

"So you really think the archfiends will get locked up again if we can stop the knights?"

Kara tried to put the ring out of everyone's minds, so no one would ask to see her to put it on her finger.

"I do." Mr. Patterson gave her a bitter smile.

"And we *must*. Because if we don't succeed, then all living things in this world and Horizon will cease to exist."

45

CHAPTER 4

HUBEI, CHINA

After a quick stop back to level three so that they could replenish their M-5 suits, Kara took the time to check with other Counter Demon Division guardians and monitors to look for signs of anything abnormal.

Now, back on Earth and while it was covered in darkness, Kara had discovered in their short stay at CDD that the most obvious anomaly had been with the farmlands. The livestock and the crops were failing and one of the biggest agricultural producers in the world was beginning to have difficulties. And even though it was largely due to the lack of sunshine, Kara couldn't overlook the darkness there. She had to check it out.

So she and her company returned to the mortal world to search for signs of the four knights of the apocalypse. And the best place to start was with the darkness in the farmlands.

Time was running out.

The guardians stood in a deep valley of rotten fields and barren meadows. The rolling hills and black mountains stretched into the darkened sky. Kara tried to picture what the scenery might have looked like in the morning sun, when the vegetation thrived in hues of gold and green, kissed by the rays of the sun. As it was, she stood on gray, withered plant life. Millions of acres of vegetation had burned and withered away. The rice crop looked like a giant ashtray.

She felt sick. It reminded her of the Netherworld, a barren, sick world of darkness and shadow. It was wrong. All of it.

"So this is China?" Kara's anger rose as she moved her boot over a black liquid that looked like ink. Most of the plants looked as if they had been doused in it.

"Actually, we're in the province of Hubei," said Peter as he bent down and examined the black liquid on a wasted plant. He rubbed it between his fingers.

"The land of fish and rice… I read that somewhere. It must have been quite beautiful before…"

"Before the archfiends did this," answered Kara angrily.

"Or should I say their little pet dogs. I bet *they* did this. It's part of their mission, right? To destroy life on earth. Well, they've already started with a bang that's for sure."

She felt David watching her. He kept glancing at her gloves, but he never asked about them, and she was thankful for it.

"It's really sad to see all this land gone to waste." Jenny knelt beside Peter and made a face.

"What is that black stuff?"

"I'm not sure." Peter brought his fingers to his nose and winced. "Smells like bile. I think it's some sort of secreted acid, maybe some sort of regurgitated substance."

"But how did it get there?" said David. "Who or *what* secreted it?"

Peter wiped his fingers on his pants. He stood up but didn't answer. They all knew the answer to that question.

As an uneasy silence passed between the guardians, Kara felt a chill crawl up her wings.

Was just one of these knights capable of such devastation? Did they wield such power?

She shuddered at the thought. Mr. Patterson had said that all things had a weakness, and she believed him. She would find it.

A faint clicking sound caught Kara's attention, like the rustling of dry leaves. But there were no leaves and no trees for miles. "That sound…do you guys hear that?"

Everyone froze.

"I don't hear anything," whispered David, breaking the silence. "What did you hear exactly?"

Kara searched the barren land and strained for the sound again, but all she could hear was the faint swishing of wind.

"I'm not sure. It's gone now, but it was like a creepy clicking sound."

"Probably just a small animal." Ashley's eyes were hard, and she didn't look convinced.

"I think this place is making us hear things." Jenny scanned the area. "I don't like the way it makes me feel. It makes me feel like death."

Kara had to agree with Jenny. There was something evil lurking somewhere. She felt it, too. Whatever it was, she felt like it was watching them. Waiting...

After another moment of silence, David said, "Probably just the wind. I wouldn't worry too much about it. Everything here is dead."

But Kara wasn't convinced. She had heard something. She was certain. But what was it?

"What's up with that smell?" Jenny moved in amongst the dead crops, her face twisted in disgust. "It's not the bile, and it's not coming from *this* field. It smells like raw sewage left out in the sun all day."

Her brow furrowed. "Smells like demons."

Kara picked up the scent. It was just to the north of where they were. Jenny was right.

Curious, and before anyone could stop her, Kara jumped into the air and stroked hard with her wings. Immediately, she soared into the air and flew toward the smell.

The smell was coming from beyond the small hillside to the north. It wasn't easy to see. Everything looked gray and in shadow. A quick glance below her and she smiled. David, Peter, Ashley and Jenny were running below her. It gave her great pleasure to be able to do something that *they* couldn't.

She would miss this, the flying, her wings. She assumed that she would return to normal once they had destroyed the knights and sent the archfiends back into their cage. The way the air rolled over her leathery wings was exhilarating. But if all worked according to plan, she would only have four days of flying left. She would get her four days' worth.

With a final bank to the left, she pulled back and arched her wings high above her head. She rolled them back and forth, her feet brushed the ground, and she landed with a slight hop. She beamed. She had landed with more grace than usual. Did the others catch that? As she turned, her smile died.

Below the hillside a vast bowl stretched beyond the horizon and disappeared into shadow. The ground was littered with the corpses of dead animals.

Thousands and thousands of cows, goats, sheep, chickens, and pigs were piled on top of one another in a giant, open grave. Their bodies were emaciated. Their skin was pulled so tight around their bodies that it was almost transparent.

How could they have died of starvation in only three days? They looked as though they had been drained of blood, of their organs, and only skin and bone remained. Even their fur and feathers had fallen off. Their eyes were empty sockets, and their bodies were stained in that same black liquid.

Kara knew they had died in pain. It was the most horrific thing she'd ever seen. It didn't feel real. It was too gruesome. No demon had the power to wreak such devastation. Only a god, a dark god, could have done this.

Instead of crying out for the fallen, Kara's rage poured through her like hot oil. She had to blink the dark spots from her eyes. She wanted to destroy the archfiends…she wanted to kill them all…

"Oh. My. God." Jenny collapsed to her knees beside Kara, her hand on her mouth. Peter knelt beside her and put his arms around her shaking shoulders.

"This is sick." David looked about as angry as Kara.

"There must be *millions* of dead animals down there. How did they all end up like this? It's like they were picked up and thrown in this valley to die. What kind of monsters could have killed so many?"

"The archfiends are as powerful as gods," said Kara. "And the four knights must have a lot of that power. It's pretty clear that *they* did this. It's their mission to destroy life so that they can break the seals for their masters."

"I don't know what I was expecting. Mr. Patterson did say they were nothing like we've ever faced before. But this…"

She lost hope. She didn't know how she could have imagined she'd be able to defeat the four knights of the apocalypse if this was any indication of what they could do. How would she defeat even a single one of them?

Kara heard that strange clicking sound again, as though someone was sharpening hundreds of knives.

"But which one did this?" asked David. "Death? It's gotta be Death."

Kara surveyed the devastation.

"I don't think it's the one called Death. This is the one called Famine. It killed the crops *and* the animals. It destroyed our source of food, and now millions of people are going to starve. Death would have left the crops and just focused on the animals."

Her face became hard as she realized the truth to her words.

"Do you think we're too late?" asked David.

Kara could only look at him.

Ashley stepped forward, a long silver sword hung in her hand. "Check your rings. We'll know if one of them is gone."

As one, David, Peter and Jenny stuck out their hands. Their golden rings glimmered on their fingers. Kara reached inside her pocket and felt around for the ring. For a horrible moment she couldn't find it. The gloves made it hard to feel anything. But then her fingertips touched something solid, and she pulled out her golden ring.

"We're not too late," she said hopefully. "The seals are all still intact. We still have time—"

Suddenly Jenny screamed.

Kara looked where Jenny was staring.

The animal corpses moved. The tangled bodies rolled and pushed awkwardly. Their limbs moved without purpose. Their stiff bodies jerked and popped like bad animation.

And just when she thought the animals were possessed and were coming back from the dead, millions of insects poured out from the mouths and eyes of the dead animals. They pushed the corpses aside as they scuttled toward the guardians like a moving carpet. Their glinting red eyes glared with eerie intelligence, and their black carapaces glimmered in the soft light.

At first Kara thought they were spiders, but then a swarm took flight like an angry black cloud. Earsplitting noise filled the air as the insects beat their wings. It sounded like knives being honed. And as they got closer, she recognized them. Locusts. Millions of locusts.

"Well, now we know where the secretions came from."

Peter glared at the wave of bugs and swung his blade around like a fly swatter. "I hate bugs."

Kara hated bugs, too, especially locusts. She hated how they used to cling to her clothes when she would go for long walks in the fields at her grandmother's cottage. She remembered the neighboring farmers complaining about how they ate entire fields of corn in a matter of hours. There was something really creepy about how much they could eat.

But these bugs looked different. They were bigger, much bigger, and they were as black as night. From what she remembered, normal locusts didn't devour animals.

"Is it me or are their beady eyes staring at us?" asked Jenny.

Ashley took a careful step back. "They're staring at us."

David cursed. "And to think that I forgot to pack my bug spray."

"I doubt bug spray would work on these," Kara said dryly. "They're not normal bugs."

The light vanished from David's eyes. "You got that right. They're more like demon bugs."

Kara watched as a cloud of bugs hovered in the air, turned, and looked as if they were preparing to attack.

"You've got a brilliant plan?"

"Nope. You?"

Kara shook her head. "No. Maybe if we walk back very slowly, they won't attack—"

The giant swarm of locusts dived at them.

"MOVE!" cried David as he spun around and ran back.

Kara just had time to drop her ring back in her pocket, before the cloud of bugs hit her like a brick wall. She went sprawling on the ground, and the locusts covered her body, clawing and biting at her skin, her wings, and her face. She beat her wings and waved her hands frantically in a panic to get the bugs off her. But there were too many. The buzzing of their wings and the chomping of their tiny mouths on her skin blocked out all other sound. They crawled up her sleeves and down through the collar of her t-shirt, all the while their teeth like thousands of death blades pierced her skin. She could feel her skin being pulled and eaten. She could feel the acid-like poison seeping inside her body. The tiny insects tore her angel skin like wild piranhas.

She thrashed out widely, like a wild, panicked animal. She was blind. She tried to pry her eyes open, but the locusts pinned her eyelids shut. She felt them biting her navel, and she panicked even more as they scrambled into her ears. When she opened her mouth to scream, more locusts climbed in.

Kara spit out the bugs, overwhelmed with terror. She felt tiny legs, like needles trying to pry open her mouth, to get in and devour her from the inside. She thought of the animals and how this was the way they must have died, eaten from the inside.

Over the constant humming in her ears, she thought she heard screaming. Was that David? Were the others under blankets of bugs? If only she could fly. Yes!

She yanked and pulled, desperately trying to open her wings. But as soon as she made to move her wings, thousands more locusts attached themselves to her, as though they could *sense* what she was about to try. Were they communicating? She shuddered at the thought of *smart* bugs.

She punched out with her arms and tried to loosen their hold on her wings. She kicked out, trying to shake them off. But it was useless. The weight of the locusts pulled her down. She couldn't fly. It was like they knew what she was about to do before she did it.

She fell, and it took tremendous effort to keep her mouth clamped shut. She was thankful she didn't need to breath. The locusts were crushing her.

She couldn't move. She couldn't scream. She couldn't think. There was only one thing left to do, something that she had sworn she wouldn't. But what else could she do?

The darkness throbbed inside her. It was like cold blood that wanted to be free. Kara had sworn never to call forth the darkness inside her or to succumb to its power. It was too dangerous. The black veins were proof. The darkness was slowly taking control of her. She would lose herself to it. What if she couldn't control it? But she couldn't let herself be eaten by bugs. It was just too lame. What kind of guardian angel dies of bug bites?

No. She wouldn't. She couldn't. She wished for her elemental power…

Jenny cried out, and it was like something inside Kara snapped.

Without thinking, she let go, and a tiny spark of dark energy pulsed through her. It was enough. With renewed strength, she jumped to her feet, thrashed her wings violently, and then spun like a top.

The locusts fell. She was surprised at how fast they came off. It was almost *too* easy. With a last loud hum, the locusts rose in a massive cloud and disappeared into the dark sky. It was almost as though something had compelled them to leave. It didn't matter. They were gone.

With a victory smile on her face, she looked back at her friends.

Jenny, Peter, Ashley and David staggered to their feet. Their faces were streaked with blood, but the locusts were gone. *Where had the locusts gone?*

Kara moved toward her friends, but a sudden fear in their eyes made her stop. They weren't looking *at* her. They were looking *past* her.

There was something behind her.

Kara whirled around, and her victory smile vanished.

A ten-foot humanoid creature sat astride a giant skeletal horse with glinting red eyes and a mouth filled with too many fish-like teeth. The horse's ribs protruded through its thin, stretched, hairless, sickly skin. So thin, it was as though its bones alone held it up. The rider's white skin looked like crumpled paper. Corded muscles sheathed its arms and legs like pale ivy. A war helmet with horns covered most of its face, and body armor covered its skeletal frame. It looked like a two-thousand-year-old mummified corpse. A gleaming black sword the size of a small tree dangled from the grip of the rider's enormous hand, and the great white horse stared at her with fiery red eyes and pointed teeth.

Kara let out gasp. She was standing face to face with one of the four knights of the apocalypse.

CHAPTER 5
FAMINE

"**W**hy didn't they tell us the knights would be giants?" grumbled David as he brandished his soul blades but then he frowned when he glanced at them. He knew that his blades wouldn't do more than scratch the giant.

"What did you expect," said Ashley, her blue eyes blazed with a fearlessness that Kara envied. "Gnomes? Dwarves? Tiny little elves?"

"Ha. Ha." David looked at Kara. "Now what? Please tell me you've packed your magic beans?"

"Magic beans?" Kara forced a laugh. "I'd go for magic. Period."

Kara didn't want to jinx it by moving just yet. The knight appeared to be contemplating what to do with them. It radiated power like a thousand heat lamps, but it was an overwhelmingly dark and evil power. Thousand-year-old intelligence gleamed in its eyes. This creature hadn't been created just three days ago. It had been around for a *very* long time.

The earth and fields seemed to pulse with its energy. The smell of rot and decay rolled off it, like a million rotted corpses. Both the rider and its steed emitted a green glow, like glowing toxic waste. Kara knew the knight controlled the atmosphere somehow. She felt a tinge of electricity prickling her wings and her skin. Abnormally low dark gray clouds with black underbellies hovered over them. The giant could probably touch them. The air was moist with the scent of rain and static. The knight's power permeated the air like the silence before an electrical storm.

A wave of terror ripped through Kara as she locked eyes with the knight. She felt its hold on her, paralyzing her with only its eyes. It didn't belong in this world. It was a dead thing, an evil thing that shouldn't be.

She did her best not to show any fear as she ransacked her mind for a plan. How to destroy this thing? Where was its weakness? She knew that this knight was Famine, and because their rings were still intact, she knew it hadn't broken the seal. Not yet. She took courage from that. Now, how to destroy it?

David leaned over and whispered. "Why isn't it moving?"

"I'm not sure," Kara whispered back, but she was certain that for whatever reason it *was* waiting, it could only be a very *bad* one.

"Maybe it's waiting for us to make the first move. But that would be stupid since I doubt our weapons would even make a scratch."

"It smells like a demon," David held his nose. "Maybe it dies like a demon."

"This is no mere demon."

A cold rage spread across Kara's face. "It feels…different…more powerful and evil. So how do we kill it?"

"I guess we're about to find out."

Kara clenched her jaw. She *would* find a way to destroy it. She had to—

"You cannot destroy me," boomed a voice that sounded like the mountains themselves were speaking.

Kara stiffened, but she planted her feet.

"Go back now, angels. Go back to the comfort and delights of your realm or you will perish along with this mortal world and everything in it."

A cold smile spread across Kara's lips. She raised her voice.

"We're not going anywhere. It is *you* that should leave, not us. We are the sworn protectors of the mortal world. We are the soldiers who drive the darkness out from this world. This world is only for the living. You have no claim here. Leave or face your doom."

The knight's red eyes shone like burning coal.

"I have already unleashed my curse upon this earth. You cannot stop the affliction. Mere angels do not possess the power to control my destruction. It will spread until all of this planet's natural resources are consumed. My plague spreads as fast and silently as the wind. It will corrupt and infect everything. The earth is already dying. You are too late."

The earth rumbled beneath Kara's feet, and she had the strangest suspicion that the knight had just laughed. It was mocking them. She suppressed a shiver.

"We're *not* too late." Kara knew that the rings were all still intact.

"We're going to send you back to whatever dimension you came from. And then the earth will heal itself. That's what she does. You might have destroyed some of the crops here in China, but they'll grow back, they always do. Life finds a way. It's obvious you don't know anything about this world because it always fights back."

The knight lowered its head, and the horns on his helmet made it look like a great bull ready to charge.

"You speak with such conviction, angel, but you know nothing about the end of days. My curse is upon your mortal world whether you'd like to admit it or not. The mortals will starve. It has already begun, and you are fools if you think you can stop me. In the end you will become like beasts and eat the flesh of other mortals."

"Okay, did he just say that we will become cannibals?" David's face was twisted in disgust.

"He did." Peter's eyes darkened. "Don't believe it. It's lying. It's trying to discourage us...to make us believe that mortals are merely animals and not worth fighting for. It wants us to let it finish what it started."

"That's not going to happen!"

Jenny looked up at the knight fiercely. "We've sworn an oath to protect the mortal world, which is what we're going to do. I don't care how scary you look. We're going to stop you."

The knight leaned back.

"Accept the inevitable. Five angels cannot stop the knights of the apocalypse. You are weak and connected to this world. You care about these mortals. You love them, and that will be your downfall. The power of the archfiends is limitless. Mere angels could never understand. My words would not be sufficient. To understand their power, you'd have to be gods yourselves."

"You're delusional," spat David. "The archfiends are not gods. They're just a bunch of god-botherers. You're all insane because you've been locked up for so long."

He leaned over and whispered in Kara's ear. "What are we doing here? We can't keep chatting forever."

"For now we have to," whispered Kara. "If we can keep it busy long enough, keep it talking, we might be able to *distract* it from its job, and it'll miss its chance to break the seal."

"But we don't even know *how* they break the seals."

"I think it has to do with how much they spread their plagues in seven days. They probably need a percentage. A certain percentage of the entire world has to succumb before the seal will break. Somehow we need to stop them from reaching that goal."

"I think we should kill it, just in case."

Kara nodded. True, if the knight were destroyed, then they'd be ahead of the game. The trouble was she wasn't sure *how* to kill it.

She returned her gaze to the creature.

"The mortals have enough gods as it is," she said, keeping their conversation going. "They don't need anymore, especially ones that want to harm them. I don't think that'll sit very well."

The knight sneered. "It makes no difference. Those who will not worship the dark gods do not deserve to live. Non-believers will die whether they are mortal or not."

"I'm pretty sure they'd disagree with you," said Kara, not fully understanding what other creatures it was referring to.

"Mortals have the right to worship any god they want. It's part of being human, to have a soul, to have an open mind and do what feels right. Who are you to decide who lives and dies?"

"The dark gods decide. They are the true gods, and they wield the power over all things."

Although the knight was terrifying, Kara was starting to get annoyed with all the talk of dark gods.

"That's a load of bull, and you know it," said David. He gave the creature a withering glare.

The knight eyed the group for a moment. "The time of angels and mortals is over. The dark gods have returned. Join us or die."

"We will never join you," spat Kara.

She was surprised at how much she trembled in rage. How dare this creature threaten her, threaten the angels and mortals, or threaten this beautiful planet. She hated its arrogant voice, so sure that it had already won. But it hadn't. The rings were proof. There was still time.

The knight cocked its head, and its thin, withered mouth stretched disgustingly into a sneer. "And yet some of you have already joined."

Kara fumed. She didn't like the way it had said *you*, as though some angels had already sided with the archfiends. No. It was lying to her.

"Your words are like poison," Kara said harshly. "But say what you want, it doesn't matter because we're the antidote, the cure for your plagues. We're going to fight you, and we're going to win."

"You think you can destroy me?" laughed the knight. "Five miserable little angels in soft angel shells? Are you ready to die your final death for this world? Your beloved legion has sent you on a fool's errand. They knew you couldn't defeat us, and still they sent you. Why is that? Do they think you are so insignificant that they are willing to sacrifice you? This is your death sentence, little ones. Why do you fight alongside a legion that cares so little for your fate?"

Kara took a step closer to it, enough to smell its foul breath. "Shut your stupid mouth, or I'll punch your teeth down your throat and shut it for you."

The knight revealed its teeth. "Your threats are empty and meaningless."

"You know nothing about us," said Kara.

The knight stared at her blankly. "I have known multitudes before you. I am a creature forged long before the time of angels. You cannot defeat me with your weapons. And when I kill you, because I *will* exterminate all of you, I will savor the moment I take your pitiful life-force because I will know how foolishly you have thrown your lives away—for a war you could never win."

The knight's horse whinnied loudly, as though it were agreeing with its master or laughing at them. It shook its head and splattered yellow and black ooze all over the ground. Despite its frail and withered body, its eyes were full of vigor. If it weren't some end-of-the-world horse, Kara would have felt sorry for it and would have fed it some hay.

"We'll see about that," murmured David.

He leaned over and whispered in Kara's ear. "If you have any great ideas about how we're supposed to defeat this thing—now's the time."

Kara looked at David. She wanted to tell him that she had some great plan, but the truth was she didn't. She had no idea how to defeat this thing. Her new wings felt small and pathetic in comparison. And for the first time, she felt completely helpless.

"Kara?" she heard Jenny whisper behind her.

But she had nothing to give. She didn't have her elemental power anymore—the one thing that could have made a real difference—and she felt overwhelmed by the weight of this burden.

She looked up and glared at the creature's red eyes anyway.

"This is your final warning, *Famine*. Yes, we know who you are. Go back to whatever world you came from, or we *will* destroy you. Whatever it takes, we're *going* to defeat you. I swear it."

Kara had no idea where she found the courage to speak to the knight like this. This was no ordinary foe. She wondered if the knights were somehow like the reapers, if their life force was linked

65

to their weapons. If these creatures had been created by the archfiends, just like the reapers, perhaps she could kill it if she disarmed it somehow. It seemed too easy. But what else could she do?

The earth shook below Kara's feet and broke her train of thought.

"The dark gods have risen once more," said the knight. "In four days and four nights, the earth will die. It will burn. And you will die with it."

Kara took a step forward, straining to hide her fear.

"This world does not belong to them or to you. It belongs to the mortals!"

The earth trembled again.

"So be it."

Just as Kara was about to yell some more, the knight raised its sword above its head. Black lightning danced on the blade, and thunder cracked. The steed neighed loudly, and black spit oozed between its sharp teeth. Kara felt a cold shiver roll down her back.

The knight grinned, and pointed its sword at them. And before she could react, before she could even blink—black tendrils shot out at each of them—all but *her*.

Her friends were encircled by the black vines. The coils of darkness tightened, and Ashley screamed as the black shadows cut into her angel flesh. Then Jenny, Peter and David howled in pain as wisps of black mist looped around them. And then something horrible happened.

They all began to wither.

Like the dead animals in the valley, their faces wrinkled, stretched, and shrunk down as though their M-5 suits had been drained of their lifeblood. They looked like hundred-year-old corpses. Their eyes lost their brilliance and became hollow, gray and glazed. Famine was draining their life force in the same way it had drained the earth of its natural resources.

"NO!"

Kara cried out. She didn't have time to ponder why the knight had spared her. She only had time to react.

Grasping her blade firmly, she stroked hard with her wings and charged at the beastly knight, aiming for its eyes. She would gouge them out.

The knight raised his other arm lazily and pointed a finger at Kara. A fist of shadows crunched into her chest, caught her in midair and spun her around. It squeezed her wings and arms together until she was cocooned in a web of black shadows. She dropped to the ground like a rock. She strained with all her strength, kicking and screaming. But she couldn't break the hold.

"Stop! I'll kill you. I'll kill you!" she cried.

She raised her head to look up at the knight. Her malice poured through her. She knew that the creature was going to kill them, and she knew that she wasn't strong enough to stop it.

Helpless, she watched in horror as her friends began to die.

CHAPTER 6
A CONNECTION

It began as a tickle in the darkness inside her, and it developed into a sudden surge of power.

Kara broke through the web of tendrils and managed to free her wings and her arms. She hacked and hacked with her sword and cut herself free.

The knight stared at her, and she recognized the surprise in his soulless, red eyes. She wasn't as weak as it had first thought. She used the knight's hesitation to her advantage.

Faster than she thought possible, Kara rocketed in the air and ploughed into the knight, putting all the weight and force she could into her attack. Crazed like a rabid animal, she thought only of death. She would kill the creature that had harmed her friends…that had harmed her David.

It worked.

She pushed her blade into the creature's left bicep and used her body weight to slice into its flesh. Black blood splattered onto her face. But at the same moment she sliced the knight's exposed flesh—*she* cried out in pain.

Kara yanked her blade out and looked down at her own arm. She had a deep laceration on her left bicep, *exactly* where she cut the creature.

She hesitated in confusion for a moment and looked up at the knight. It stared back at her and smiled evilly, exposing its mouth full of black needle-like teeth. Then it backhanded her with a brutal blow that sent her flying.

She lay sprawled in pain. She was dazed and unable to wrap her head around what had just happened.

Before she had a chance to gather herself again, she felt strong arms lift her to her feet. It was David.

She whimpered slightly in her confusion. David looked a little disheveled, but otherwise he bore no signs of Famine's wrath. His handsome face was back to normal. She collected her wits and inspected the others. They appeared to be unscathed and safe, for the moment.

"What just happened?"

David let go of Kara and looked from Kara to the creature.

"I think...I think I injured it. I stabbed it, and it broke the connection somehow."

Kara's sudden fit of stupid-fury had worked. But she didn't have time get into the details. Her friends were safe. She could work with that. She turned around slowly and faced the knight again.

She gave him a giant smile and challenged him, "Is that all you've got, knight of the apocalypse?"

She did her best to hide the terror she felt. Something had happened between her and the knight, something that felt wrong and terrifying.

She looked at the knight's wound as she brushed her fingers over the corresponding wound on her arm.

How was this possible? What did it mean? Why wasn't the knight retaliating?

The knight had a clear shot now. It only had to swing its giant sword, and she would be sliced in half. But the knight had a strange calmness in its eyes, like it knew something. *But what?*

Something had definitely passed between them.

Kara steadied herself and resisted the urge to jump in again. She hated the knight more than ever now, but she didn't want to have any sort of *connection* to this demon. She wanted to gouge its eyes out, to make it stop watching her. She couldn't explain it, but she knew the knight knew exactly what she was thinking. It *knew* what had happened.

If they were connected, what did that really mean? If she killed the knight, would she die, too?

David was watching her closely. If she weren't careful, he would figure out that she and the knight had identical wounds, that somehow they were linked.

"What?" she taunted the knight in spite of her fears.

"You scared now? You should be. Didn't think I could get that close, did you? Next time, it'll be your throat."

"Kara, what are you doing?" hissed David.

"Making it angry."

"It was already angry."

She took a step closer. She hated this creature for the fear it caused inside her. If she were indeed connected to this monster, she would have to cut it from her.

Angling her body as she had trained, she readied to push off hard and attack again. It didn't matter if she and this thing were bonded somehow. She would cut off its head.

As her hatred pulsed inside her body, Kara leaped into the air.

The knight opened its mouth.

She halted.

It opened its jaws abnormally wide until its chin rested on the back of its steed. Kara could hear humming emanating from somewhere deep inside the creature's throat. It sounded like thousands of drums beating.

And just when things couldn't get any worse, masses of locusts shot out of its maw like bullets from a machine gun.

The locusts swarmed and circled the guardians. But just when Kara thought they were going to attack again, the locusts separated into groups. The locusts in each group drew themselves together, and Kara could see that they were transforming themselves into something. They were forming humanoid figures. Locust-men!

"What in the souls do you call those?" Jenny swung her bow over her shoulder and nocked an arrow.

"I don't think there's an actual word for those," cried Peter. He parried with his blade dodging invisible blows.

"I don't care what they're called, as long as we can *kill* them." Ashley advanced with her sword clasped securely.

"I'm with Ashley." David gave Kara a sidelong glance.

But Kara wasn't watching the bug-men. She was glaring at the knight.

"Coward!" she bellowed. "Fight us! Fight me!"

Fury fuelled her. She could hardly see the knight, who appeared to be hiding behind the wall of bug-men. Perhaps it knew she was the only one who could kill it. Maybe it even *feared* her. She needed to cut her connection with this monster and find out, once and for all, if she'd kill herself in the process.

There was no time to think.

The locust-men steadied themselves and then charged.

"Get ready!" was all Kara could voice before a locust-man launched itself at her. With a beat of her wings she leaped from the ground, but not fast enough.

The locust-man caught her leg, and with an incredible force for a thing made of just insects, it yanked her down.

Kara beat her wings feverishly, but another locust creature grabbed her other leg. Their grip was like thousands of needles pricking into her skin. The creatures tossed her sprawling to the ground.

They came at her again, but Kara was already up.

"You're going to pay for that."

She launched herself at a locust-man, spinning and driving a sidekick in the creature's chest. The locust-man exploded in a stink of vomit and sewage.

But the locusts reformed, and the locust-man came at her again. She kicked out hard and landed another blow, this time to the creature's head. Again the locusts shattered, but as quickly as they had split apart they reformed, as though nothing had happened.

Out of the corner of her eye, she caught a glimpse of the knight. Famine sat on his emaciated steed and watched them with a bored and irritated expression, as though he already knew that he and his insect army would win.

Kara cursed loudly. If she wanted to be a normal angel again, if she wanted to stop her transformation, she *had* to stop the knight from breaking the seal. But she had no idea how she was going to do that. Great.

She soared up into the air and hovered for a moment as she tried to figure out what to do next. She pulled her soul blade from the folds of her jacket. It was a guess really, as she didn't know if it would affect the creature, but she had to try something.

A locust-man cocked its head, as though it was considering whether or not the blade was a threat. For a moment she thought she saw it flash a smile.

The creature charged at her like a rocket. She swerved and slashed across its rippling insect chest with the tip of her blade. Handfuls of locusts fell from their humanoid host, like burned skin peeling off a body. A screeching buzz sounded from the creature, as though it screamed in pain.

Kara could see that David was holding his own against two locust-men, slashing at them with a soul blade in each hand. But each time he drove his blade into a creature's chest, although the locusts exploded into clouds of swarming insects, they reformed within a few seconds.

Jenny and Ashley weren't doing any better.

Ashley spun and sliced skillfully with her sword, slicing two creatures at once, and Jenny nocked arrow after arrow and hit her mark every time. But the creatures always reformed.

She spotted Peter and was surprised as he, too, held his own. But then two of the locust-men ganged up on him, and he disappeared under flailing, insect claws. *Peter!*

She made to swoop to Peter's aid, but something pinned her wings from behind.

She smelled the bile and heard the buzzing wings of a locust-man as it pulled at her wings. She cried out in pain as some locusts broke free and tore at her M-5 suit. She thrashed out with her blade but missed. The locust man held her wings tight, and she plummeted from the sky.

Kara hit the ground hard, but luckily she had squished the locust-creature in the process.

She rolled and pushed herself up. But just as she almost smiled at her luck, another locust-man punched her in the face. Her head snapped back. White lights exploded behind her eyelids. She staggered, and another blow hit her in the stomach. Locusts scrambled into her eyes, blinding her. Her head snapped around as another blow caught her on the side of the head.

From the corner of her eye she saw the knight open its jaws. Another swarm of locusts flew out, and fifty more locust-men formed and attacked.

She leaped at her attacker, only to be grabbed from the back again. A second locust-man leaned in, smiled a contorted locust grin, pulled back its arm, and curled it into a fist. Then it punched Kara in the stomach, like a shot from a cannon. She felt her angel shell shatter as the creature's fist punctured her stomach.

The creature pulled back its hand, and light seeped from the deep wound in her chest. Even before she gasped at the piercing pain, she felt the scurrying and digging of tiny feet inside her body. The locusts had infected her.

"Kara!" she heard David shout, terrified.

But she hardly heard him. Her own terror had overtaken her.

She felt the insects spreading as they multiplied inside her. Kara screamed in utter terror as the locusts began to feast on her angel essence. She staggered as more locusts crawled around her face, and she felt herself weakened by their poison. She was vaguely aware that three more locust-men had begun to assault her.

Dimly, she heard Jenny cry out.

Then she heard a scream that she recognized as Ashley's. *Were they being infested as well?* Three locust-men held Ashley down, and Kara could see Ashley's angel essence pouring out from many tiny cuts.

Jenny was on her knees, screaming and crying as she punched and slashed at the five locust-men that came at her.

Kara was overwhelmed. They couldn't keep fighting like this. She couldn't see or hear any signs of David or Peter.

David…

She felt her own strength evaporate. Her legs shook, and she collapsed. The locusts were inside her, eating her essence and spreading their poison. She couldn't move or fight. It had happened so fast. And there was nothing she could do but lie down and wait to die.

CHAPTER 7

A LITTLE BIT OF DARKNESS

Her vision had blurred, and she was about to pass out when she felt the ripple of a little spark inside her. At first she thought the locusts had finally reached her soul, but then she felt it again. This was different, like an electrical charge, like a battery being recharged—her battery.

It was like her body had turned on its self-defense mode, and even though she had not called upon it, the darkness inside began to assert itself. It wouldn't let her die.

Her body jerked as the cold, rippling darkness sent shockwaves through her. Her wings tingled. Her cold power flowed more forcefully. Her fingers curled, clawing into the dirt. The power terrified her, but it was also intoxicating. She lost control to the dark force so quickly that she wasn't even aware what had happened.

The darkness churned inside her, and her fingers pulsed with a new energy. Strong energy.

It was the same sensation of dark power she had felt before, that wild forbidden power that had whispered to her and teased her. It wanted her to succumb to it, to set it free. She feared and embraced it as she felt it pulse from the tip of her wings and through her body. And although she knew she'd be lost to it now that she couldn't control the force that was taking her over, she didn't care.

It had saved her. And now she would *save* her friends.

Kara groaned, and as she stood up hundreds of dead locusts poured out of the deep wound in her stomach like waste. Black veins spread over her chest and pulled her wound together, stitching it up like medical thread until she was completely healed. Except for the hole in her shirt and the black veins that covered her upper body, it was as though the locust-man had never punched her at all. The last locust scurried over her face and tried to pry her lips open, but she bit it in half and spit out the bug's guts.

She felt her power surge. It pulsed in her hands and legs. She was going to kill them all.

With bloodlust in her eyes, she spotted Famine. It was looking straight at her, and for a horrible moment, it seemed *happy*.

She didn't have time to wonder why it looked so smug. She had to help out her friends first. The knight would be next on her to-kill list.

Kara spread her wings and jumped into the air. Masses of locust-men had overpowered her friends like a sand storm. Jenny lay crumbled beneath a swarm of locusts. Ashley was a few feet away, and Kara could see her angel essence seeping from her many wounds as she fought the creatures with her bare hands.

Kara dove toward Jenny. She spun around with a powerful beat of her wings so violent that the blast of wind flung the locust-men into the air and splatted them onto the ground in a black and green mess. Then she spun like a top, spreading out her wings like a razorblade tornado. The edges of her wings hacked, sliced, shredded through the locust-men like a revolving meat grinder. Insect blood and guts fell like heavy rain.

She was lost in a fury of hatred, in her hunger to kill, and she kept killing until she had annihilated every last locust creature.

"Kara, stop!"

Kara halted, but the darkness still pulsed inside her. It wanted her to kill again and again. She knew in that moment that it would never leave her, not anymore. She had broken *its* seal.

David ran up to her. He surveyed the severed bugs and then stared at her for far too long. His face hardened, and his eyes narrowed. Why was he looking at her like that? Hadn't she just saved them? Shouldn't he be thanking her?

Peter was lifting Jenny to her feet. She was battered, but in much better shape than Kara would have thought. Ashley stood next to them with her sword in her hand and a murderous look on her pretty face. Her friends were safe. All of them. Strangely enough, she felt great.

The earth rumbled slightly, and Kara's sudden heroic feeling died like the bugs at her feet. She spun on the spot.

"Where's the knight?"

"Gone," said David. He was still looking at her with a perplexed expression as he moved closer to her.

Kara felt deflated and furious. They had lost their chance at killing it. *She* had lost her chance. She feared what had been revealed between her and the knight. She didn't understand the truths that she so desperately wanted to know. Where did it go and why?

"The bugs," she squished a few dead locusts underfoot. "They were a diversion for a quick getaway. They kept us busy while it continued to spread its wickedness."

She looked quickly at her injured bicep. The wound had healed, but it didn't make her feel any better.

"Well, I don't know exactly when the knight packed up and left, but it was around the time you went all DEET on the bugs." David stood right in front of her now, but there was no love or kindness in his eyes, only fear.

"What?" said Kara.

David was not supposed to look at her that way. At first she thought he was looking at her arm, but his eyes remained fixed on her *face*.

"Is it the bugs?" Kara watched for his reaction. But there was none.

"Do I still have bug guts all over my face or something?" She wiped her face with her sleeve.

"Is it gone now? What is it, seriously? Stop staring at me like that and just *tell* me."

The others were staring at her, too.

"Your face," began Jenny. She looked at Kara's face like it was the ugliest thing she'd ever seen. "It's all...it's all..."

"It's all *what?*" Kara felt the darkness start to rise in her. It wanted to be released again, but she pushed it down.

What was wrong with them all? They should be grateful that she had risked her angel life to rescue them, not pass judgment on her.

"I can clean it off later," Kara growled.

"That's not it." Kara wasn't surprised that Ashley should have a compact mirror. She tossed it to Kara.

"You're all covered in like black veins or something like that. See for yourself. Take a look."

Kara caught the mirror and looked at her face. It was her worst fear.

Like deep black tattoos, the veins covered her face like crawling vines. They extended from her neck, all the way up her cheeks, to her forehead.

Kara tossed the mirror on the ground. She turned away from her friends and hid her grotesque face with her hands. She shook in fear and shame. It was her fault. She had let the darkness in, and now there was no going back.

How could she have been so stupid? So careless? The white oracle had warned her that she could change the future. But now her future seemed to be set in stone.

She looked like a monster because she was about to become one.

Part of her wanted to cry. A good mortal cry had always made her feel better. But she wasn't mortal anymore. She wasn't even an angel. There was no point in crying. All she could feel was anger.

"Kara?" asked David softly. "What's going on? What are those markings?"

She opened her mouth to answer him, but her voice wouldn't come, and she cursed herself silently.

"Did you know this would happen? Please, tell me what's happening to you," he pleaded.

When he saw the terror in her eyes, he continued with a touch of humor. "I promise I won't laugh, even if you do look like you belong at the circus."

God she loved him. She wanted to smack him for the last comment, too, but she just loved how he always tried to make her laugh in sensitive situations. She didn't deserve such a good friend. But all that would change when she'd turned into a monster. Would she even remember his face?

David moved around her, but she kept her face hidden with her hands.

"Is that why you've been wearing gloves? Because of this? There are more of these veins, aren't there? If it's on your face now, then it's all over your body, too. Your secret is out, Kara. You can't hide anymore. Tell us. Tell us what's going on."

David wasn't accusing her in any way. He was surprisingly cool and comforting.

Finally, Kara pulled her hands away from her face. She longed for some tears, god how she longed for a really good cry. She nodded slowly, still unable to speak. She pulled her gloves off and felt the others watching her. She was inflicted with an incurable disease. She was corrupted, and it would only get worse.

She tossed the gloves on the ground and raised her hands for all to see, but she didn't look at them. She was afraid that they would be disgusted with her, and she was ashamed.

But what happened next, she didn't expect.

Instead of looks of repulsion and fear, they looked at each other and then tackled her into a group bear hug.

It was too much.

Kara's lips wavered. Her knees were weak, and she was barely aware of the little cry that escaped her lips as her friends hugged her tighter. She could feel their love and their loyalty. It was if they knew exactly what she needed. She needed them, and she hugged them back.

Finally, as everyone drew back, she found it hard to look at them. They had never really shared such intimacy before, not like this. But now she felt empowered because she had the support of her friends.

David still had his arms around her waist. She raised her eyes to his, and he said with an impish smile, "Your body could be covered in green scales for all I care. It doesn't matter. It won't change how I feel about you."

Kara bit down on her bottom lip. She had never expected him to make such a strong declaration of his feelings in front of everyone. She knew her friends had figured out how she and David felt about one another, but it had always been an unspoken understanding. He had just never announced it in such an affirmative way before.

"You're still my Kara."

Kara shook her head, "You're impossible."

Kara couldn't help herself. She burst out laughing and pushed him away playfully. Her smile was as wide as the fields. She couldn't find the right words to thank them. Maybe she didn't need to.

"Well, the knight is definitely gone," said David. "Our chances of finding him now don't look so great. He'll know we'll be looking for him, and he'll make it harder for us to find him, I guarantee it."

Kara's smile faded. "Maybe, but we still need to find him. We'll just have to look harder because he'll need to destroy a lot more crops and animals to break the seal. We'll follow the trail of death that follows him, and we'll find him, I'm sure we will. It's only a matter of time. He couldn't have gotten too far even if he is supernatural."

As Kara surveyed the hectares of dead and diseased crops and animals, she wondered what she would do when she faced the knight again. Could she kill him without injuring herself further? She thought about asking Mr. Patterson what he thought the connection was. If anyone knew details about the knights, she trusted that he would. And she wouldn't make the same mistake of hiding anything from anyone, not anymore.

"Well, whatever we *do* decide to do, we better hurry," said Jenny.

She looked at her wristwatch. "The day's almost over. If we don't find him soon and destroy him, it'll only leave us three days to find and kill all four of them. We don't have much time. And if the other knights are as strong as him—"

"I'm sure they are," interrupted Ashley. She twirled her sword in the air like she was slicing invisible locusts. "They're probably worse."

Jenny shrugged. "Then we haven't really made any real progress at all."

"We just got our butts kicked," grunted Peter. He pulled off his glasses and began to wipe off the caked on bug guts with the bottom of his t-shirt.

"We need to do better. If the knights are this strong, I hate to image the strength of their creators. Can you image what they'll do to the legion of angels? Mr. Patterson was right—they'd annihilate them. It's up to us to stop the knights from breaking the seals."

"Praying that the old man's plan will actually *work*," said David.

He saw the irritated looks they were all giving him. "What? He said *believed!* You were there, you all heard him. Even *he's* not entirely sure his grand plan's going to work."

"We'll make it work." Peter pushed his glasses back on his face.

"Kara made it work, right, Kara? We all saw it. The creature let us go. You did something to it didn't you? What was it?"

"I injured it," she answered.

Peter's eyes gleamed. "How did you manage that?"

"Well, I can't really say that I injured it because I doubt that very much. It was more of a surprise. I caught it off guard and sliced it across the arm with my blade. It happened really fast and to tell you the truth I'm not even sure how it let me get so close. But I did. Maybe it was too busy trying to kill you all and didn't see me coming. The cut wasn't very deep, but it must have been painful enough to break the hold it had on you guys."

She couldn't bring herself to tell them about the wound that had appeared on her own arm, at least not until it made more sense. She'd speak to Mr. Patterson first.

"So that's great," said Jenny cheerfully. "At least one of us achieved something today."

Kara's face was blank. "Don't get too excited. I would hardly call this an achievement. I surprised it, that's all. I doubt that the knight will let me get that close to it again."

David let out a long sigh and looked to the sky. He sheathed his blades inside his jacket. "Well, it *can't* get any worse than this."

"Oh, it gets worse," said Ashley. Everyone turned to look at her. She pointed her sword at Peter's hand.

Jenny's eyes widened. "Oh, no. Peter, your ring!"

Peter lifted his ring hand. His ring was gone.

The first seal had been broken.

CHAPTER 8
SECRETS AND LIES

It was with a feeling of dread that Kara and the others travelled back to Horizon. They had failed to stop Famine from breaking his seal. The archfiends were getting closer to their victory.

Kara hid in the shadows while she waited for the rest of the group to be released from the archangel Raphael's care. They were fine, but protocol demanded that they get checked out anyway. She refused to get checked, partly because she felt fine, but mostly because she didn't want to draw attention to herself. She had to agree with David. She looked like a freak show all on her own. Ultimately, she would seek Mr. Patterson's council *first*, and then she'd decide whether or not to let the rest of the legion in on the progress of her transformation. Would they even care? They were on the brink of war. Perhaps they wouldn't even notice.

Time was passing. After spending a few hours in Horizon to repair their injuries, they had only three days left.

Kara waited for her friends in a long corridor opposite the hallway from Raphael's chamber. A group of middle-aged CDD agents came strutting down the corridor, and Kara stepped back deeper into the shadows and flattened herself against the stone wall.

"…who sent them on this mission anyway," said a man's voice.

"I checked the chart, and no field missions assigned to anyone. What the heck were they doing? Don't they know it's pointless? We could really use the extra manpower. Gabriel said it would be the biggest battle the legion had ever seen. They should be fighting alongside us tomorrow when we hit the archfiends."

Kara frowned but crept a little closer to hear more.

"There was no *official* mission," said a woman's voice. "It was the one with the demon wings, the *freak*. No doubt she orchestrated all of this to bring more attention to herself. She lied to her team and nearly got them all killed. She's always been a real problem with the legion. She makes everyone uneasy. Cathy in Operations told me that she was supposed to be *terminated* last year."

"No way," said one of the men.

Kara's mood darkened. She clenched her fists.

"I swear it on the souls," the woman's voice rose with excitement.

"There's something *foul* about her. I just know it. She's corrupted, and she corrupts everyone around her, like a bad apple. I honestly don't know why they keep her around. If it were up to me, I'd get rid of her."

"Well, it's not up to you."

"Her team is going to die because of her, you just watch," said the woman.

"If they're stupid enough to follow that freak," said another man's voice.

"Then they're stupid enough to die along with her." The voices laughed.

"I wouldn't be sorry if she did die," the woman snorted. "We don't need mutants like that here. She doesn't belong in Horizon. They should have left her locked up in Tartarus. Or better yet...fed her soul to the demons."

The all laughed as they went past Kara.

She stepped out of the shadows. She wanted to shout at them, to tell them off. It took every ounce of strength to keep from dive-bombing the three of them and slapping them around with her wings. She'd show them how much of a *freak* she was. She had to tell herself that these were ignorant fools.

But they didn't appear to know anything about the seals; otherwise they would have said so. No. It was clear that her mission was a secret one. She might look like a freak, but she was important enough to Mr. Patterson, and hopefully some of the other archangels, to entrust her on this secret and vital mission.

"Idiots," she said under her breath.

"Well, well, well. What do we have here, ladies?"

Kara froze. And then she cursed. Even before she turned around, she knew who it was. She kept her head hidden in the shadows of her hood and turned around.

"Kara Nightingale," said Metatron between puffs of his cigar. "The one with the mark—or should I say the one with the *wings*."

He looked exactly as she had tried hard to forget. His charcoal-gray suit was a bit tight around the middle, and his thin, straw-colored hair was drawn back from his receding hairline. He hid his eyes behind his glasses, but she knew he watched her with great interest. He was oily, like a gangster lord, full of false promises, full of criminal resolve and evil secrets.

His entourage of stunning angel woman in skin-tight, black leather suits, red high heels, sunglasses, and bright red lipstick stood in his shadow.

Kara held back a growl.

"Why are you hiding?" he laughed as he tapped the ashes from his cigar.

"With such a pretty face like yours I'm surprised you're not flaunting it around."

He glanced toward the group of guardians who had just passed. A knowing smile spread on his lips.

"I wasn't hiding."

Metatron laughed harder. "But you *are* hiding. But the question is why? And from whom are you hiding?"

The archangel's laughter only made Kara's fury bubble even more. He was a rude and arrogant fool who still thought it was cool to smoke cigars. She hated him and his stupid entourage. Their sweet cherry-blossom and vanilla perfume was giving her a giant headache.

"Leave me alone," growled Kara. She remembered who she was speaking to and added, "Please."

Metatron's face twitched.

"Remember who you're speaking to, guardian," he warned with a dangerous edge to his voice. "I'm not some mindless, spineless archangel. I'm your commander, and you'd do well to remember that."

Kara wasn't about to apologize. Maybe if she ignored him, he'd get bored and walk away.

Metatron smiled.

"Come, come, Kara. Aren't we friends? Of course we are. Let me gaze upon that pretty face of yours."

But Kara didn't budge.

"Come here now," he ordered. "I won't say it again."

Kara had been caught by the worst archangel in all Horizon. Why couldn't it have been Raphael? She cursed herself for not going with the others.

She took a step forward and kept her head down. But she knew he was close enough to see the markings on her face.

"Oh dear," said Metatron.

Smoke from his cigar billowed into her face. "It's worse than I expected. You *have* been busy."

She raised her head slowly and angrily and stared into his sunglasses. The entourage gasped, but she ignored them.

"You know this isn't my fault. I never asked for any of this."

Kara caught her reflection in his sunglasses and froze for a moment. The shock of the thick, black veins tattooed on her face was still very fresh. She didn't like the monster that stared back at her. She looked away and hid under her hood.

Metatron took a drag of his cigar. She hated that she couldn't see his eyes.

"Maybe not," he said, and then he was quiet for a while. "But it's happened, hasn't it?"

Even though she couldn't see his eyes, she knew he was taking in *everything*.

And then Metatron said finally, "Your transformation seems to be progressing faster than I had expected."

"This *complicates* things," he said to himself.

What things? Kara wanted to ask.

"How are you *feeling?*" he asked.

Kara thought that it was an odd question, coming from him.

"Does it hurt? Are you in any kind of pain? Do you have a fever?"

"Fever? No. I feel fine." Kara glared at one of his entourage who was openly staring and laughing at her.

Metatron took another drag of his cigar. To her surprise, he blew a butterfly.

"You certainly don't *look* fine. Such a pity. You had such a pretty face."

He was silent again, and Kara had the feeling that he knew more than he let on.

"I feel fine," she repeated. She couldn't let him remove her from her mission. She needed to save herself, as well as the world.

"I can still do my job, if that's what's worrying you. Nothing's changed—"

"Except for those black marks all over you." His eyes rolled over her body too long.

Kara controlled her temper. "It doesn't affect my skills as a guardian. I'm just as good as I was before, even better because of the wings. I'm a real asset to the legion and to my team. My—my *condition* won't affect my work. I promise."

The women snorted at this. She wanted to slice off their pretty heads.

The archangel gave her a sly smile. "It's already affecting your work if you feel the need to hide in the shadows. You can't hide your wings anymore, and you certainly can't hide your face."

He flicked his cigar toward her. "You say that your wings are an asset, so why do you shy away like you're ashamed of them?"

"I'm not." Kara contracted her hands into fists and concentrated hard to keep the darkness from taking her over.

Metatron's smile faded a little.

"Only the guilty shy away from others, those who do not wish to share their secrets, those who do not want to be discovered. Tell me. Are you guilty of something, Kara? What shameful incident have you done that makes you lurk in the shadows?"

"I haven't done anything," she said coldly.

"Really?" Metatron shared smiles with his entourage. It made Kara want to vomit.

He turned his attention back to her and took a long drag from his cigar.

"From where I'm standing, it sure looks like you're hiding something. I told you before, I can always tell when someone is lying…and you, my dear, are lying. It's all over your *face*."

Kara flinched.

"I'm *not* lying. I haven't *done* anything. I'm just standing here waiting for my team. I don't recall any laws against lurking in the hallways."

"A tongue like a razor. I like that. I find it very charming in someone so young."

Kara made a face.

"We all have our secrets—though I'm curious why you're so jumpy. If I were a fool, I'd say you can keep your secrets. But I am no fool. And keeping secrets from the legion, from me, is a capital offense. I could send you straight to Tartarus without questions or a hearing."

"Fine," she spat, before she knew what she was saying, before she could control her temper. "Send me to your prison! See if I care. But if you're so sure I've done something wrong then why haven't you sent me to Tartarus already?"

She narrowed her eyes, surprised at her courage or stupidity to be speaking with such impertinence to the archangel. The darkness was making her mad.

"I'll tell you. It's because you've got *nothing*. Because I haven't done anything."

To her amazement Metatron laughed. "You're so feisty and insolent, such anger in that tiny little body. It's one of the reasons why I like you so much, and why I haven't sent you to

Tartarus…yet. It's because I like you, and I like having you around. There are not many angels who have the nerve to speak to me like you just did. In fact I don't recall it happening for over three hundred years…and come to think of it, he's still in Tartarus."

Kara's throat tightened as she remembered the heart wrenching echoes of lost souls she'd heard during her stay in the angel prison and wondered if she'd had heard that poor, forgotten angel's cry. How could Metatron forget an angel for three hundred years in that despicable place? It only made her hate him more. Why would the legion appoint such a ruthless, uncaring commander? It was crazy.

Metatron smiled at her grimace.

"I admire a guardian who's not afraid to speak her mind. It sets you apart. But like I said, not always in a good way. Lucky for you, I find you amusing."

"Wonderful." Kara stepped back into the shadow of the corridor and fought back the scream that she held inside her. If he did anything to prevent her from becoming a normal angel again, she'd feed him his cigar.

"Amusing, yes, but also significant." Metatron sidled closer to her and brushed her wings with his fingers. Her skin crawled at his nearness, but she didn't move an inch.

"Truly, your wings are remarkable," continued the archangel. "But these…these veins tell a different story, don't they?"

Kara was restless, but at the same time remarkably still. Was he aware of the darkness that brewed inside her? How much did Mr. Patterson and the oracles tell the legion about what they saw in her future?

Perhaps he didn't know…not yet.

"What is their purpose?" he asked sweetly, standing too close to her. His breath was like an ashtray. "Why are they there at all? Are they trying to tell us something? What does it all mean?"

Kara's brows knotted. "Your guess is as good as mine."

She wouldn't tell *him* anything. He would have to beat it out of her. *God, why can't he just go away?*

Metatron watched her in silence for a moment.

"Well, I'm sure whatever they are they will reveal their mystery soon enough. They don't seem to pose any kind of threat that I can see…for the moment. Either way, I've allowed you to stay in the legion until we discover more about these dreadful marks."

"Thanks, I'm sure."

Something shifted in the reflection of Metatron's glasses, his smile flattened. "You are remarkably *ungrateful*."

That was too much.

"Ungrateful? I'm *ungrateful?*"

Now she was yelling. "After everything that's happened to me? Over and over and over again without being able to stop it, without being able to say no! I've never asked to have elemental power! I've never asked for these wings…these marks. I've never even asked to be an *angel*. It just happened, and I had no say in it. And was I ungrateful for all of this? For all these things that keep happening to me? No. I've always only shown my appreciation and my devotion to the cause because I believe in it. Even if it doesn't believe in me. I've always been grateful. I do my job to the best of my ability, and

I've saved countless mortal and angel lives. If that's ungrateful, then shoot me."

Kara shook with rage. She'd carried these feelings with her for so long, and now they had exploded out of her. Her only regret was that she had unleashed them on Metatron, the one who really could send her away forever.

The female entourages' smiles had disappeared completely. Their pretty faces looked stunned. They watched Metatron and waited. No one moved. No one said a word. The fact that they weren't laughing at her sudden outburst was an answer in itself—she had gone too far. Metatron would never let this go, especially in front of his groupies. He would punish her severely.

Kara braced herself.

He tapped the ashes from his cigar.

"Well, someone forgot to take their happy pills this morning." He stared at her sullenly. "I'm feeling generous today, so I'm going to pretend I didn't hear any of this juvenile tantrum. Because, that's what it was, wasn't it? A tantrum, brought on by stress, no doubt."

When Kara realized he was waiting for her to answer, she said, "Yes, yes I guess you're right. I should be grateful to you."

Why wasn't he angrier with her?

He looked almost sad. She couldn't see his eyes, but it was clear now. He felt sorry for her, and she felt angry again. She didn't want anyone's pity, especially not his.

Metatron studied her for a long time and then added. "Where's your beloved Davy? The two of you are usually inseparable, like two peas in a pod, right?"

He laughed and raised his eyebrows. "So what does he think about your latest look? Is he more or less inclined to be with you? By the looks of it, I'm going to guess less."

Kara knew he was only trying to get a rise out of her, and she wouldn't play his game. So instead she asked, "I heard the legion's planning a strike on the archfiends tomorrow. I'm sure you're very busy with plans and all. I wouldn't want to keep you from such an important thing."

She wasn't expecting him to answer, but she figured she had nothing to lose.

Metatron frowned. "You heard? Ariel didn't inform you? That's not like her."

Kara's face fell. Obviously he didn't know about their mission, and she was about to ruin everything with her big mouth.

"Yes. Of course she did," she lied quickly.

"We're all getting ready, physically and mentally. It's just..."

She faltered and cursed herself for being so stupid. There was no *official* mission. Mr. Patterson had sent them out himself, out of desperation, without the legion's knowledge. The legion hadn't accepted his theory about the seals and the knights. But now Kara and the others were in dangerous territory—they had been on a secret and unauthorized mission.

For a moment she felt elated. She had never been one to follow the rules when breaking them was much more thrilling.

Still, Mr. Patterson should have warned them.

"It's just what?" demanded the archangel.

"I thought maybe...I was hoping maybe you could stop it."

"Stop it? Have you lost your mind?" Metatron's face hardened.

"I *don't want* to stop it. And why would I? We need to hit these archfiends with everything we've got. They're a threat to us and to the mortal world. These creatures want to *annihilate* us. Do you know what that means?"

"Of course I do." Kara straightened and resisted the urge to snap back, his foul mood was increasing by the millisecond.

"We *must* destroy them before they get a chance to attack first. There's no other alternative. We're going to hit them hard. With the demon legions fighting alongside us, the archfiends won't stand a chance. It'll all be over in less than a few hours. I guarantee it. I'm confident we *will* win this."

"And you seriously *trust* the demons?" Kara did her best to hide the skepticism in her voice.

Metatron went still, and a shadow passed over his face.

"No, I don't trust any demon and I never will. But I trust that they need to vanquish the archfiends as much as we do. They stand to lose as much as us if things turn out badly. The archfiends have no love for the demons either. If they don't destroy the Netherworld, then they will bend it to their will. The enemy of my enemy is my friend."

"It just doesn't feel right. They can't be trusted."

"There is no other way—"

"But there *is* another way."

Kara moved forward. She forgot the marks on her face and ignored the stares of Metatron's entourage.

"The demons have an ulterior motive. I know they do. They'll turn on us, on you. Maybe they want us to die, I don't know. But you can't let the legion strike the archfiends now. They'll never win!"

Her voice rose. "They'll be killed if you don't stop it. The archfiends will slaughter the angels! All of them."

The words rushed out of her mouth. "You must stop them. Please. There'll be nothing left! They're more powerful than anything in this world. I've only seen a glimpse of what they're capable of—"

She shut her mouth. She had said too much. The secret was out.

"A glimpse?" Metatron's voice became deeper and more authoritative. Kara shuddered slightly under the power of his stare. His entourage stepped back.

"What *glimpse* are you referring to?"

"Well, it's more of a feeling than a literal glimpse," she lied. She wanted to kick herself. "Call it angel intuition. I get it from time to time, and I'm usually right."

"Are you now?" Metatron's face was unreadable.

"You've been speaking to that oracle again, haven't you? What's that one's name again? *Mr. Patterson*, that's the name. What do oracles know of combat and warfare? Of battles? What do oracles know of military strategies? Nothing. They've never really partaken in any wars. They've never fought side by side with angels. They spend their days scrying through crystal balls! Crystal balls! They don't know the first thing about battles or how to win the war against the archfiends. And instead of filling young minds with foolish ideals of war, they should stick to fortune telling."

Kara knew she had struck a nerve. She guessed that Mr. Patterson and the other oracles had interfered with the legion's war plans over the centuries. Was Metatron opposed to the oracle's recommendation to go after the knights of the apocalypse? She hoped she hadn't made this more difficult for Mr. Patterson.

"I will have a talk with that old fool and set him straight once and for all."

Kara was stuck. There was nothing she could say to help Mr. Patterson without revealing too much about their mission.

Metatron's oily stare fixed on her again. He clicked his tongue. "This just won't do."

"Excuse me?"

The archangel moved away from her. "Your face, those marks, your wings...all of it. It's clear to me now. This causes a problem for our *deal*."

Kara winced. The infamous deal.

She hadn't forgotten about it, but she hadn't really thought it was relevant any more. Metatron had agreed not to torture David because he wanted to get information from her. He had offered her a deal in exchange for David's safety, and she had taken it. She had never told anyone, not even to David. She had hoped that the archangel had forgotten about it. Cleary he hadn't.

But did he just say that there was a problem?

Kara couldn't stand this any longer. If he hadn't been the overall legion commander, and if she hadn't been linked to him because of the deal they had made, she would have punched him.

"Yes, our deal," he purred. "You do remember our deal, don't you?"

Kara clenched her jaw. She wanted to scream. This was insufferable.

"I could have overlooked the wings," he continued. He took a long drag from his cigar, "But I can't have you looking like *that* around me."

Gray smoke billowed from his lips. "It would make my *girls* uncomfortable."

Kara looked over to his entourage. They leered at her. Their red, bulbous lips were turned up in smiles that were not friendly.

"So…regrettably…and I mean it in the most sincere way because you *were* quiet beautiful…"

Kara leaned forward. She was going to punch him.

Metatron tapped his cigar. "The deal's off."

Kara felt relief, anger, and ultimately, excitement. This couldn't have happened at a better time.

It was odd. She thought she heard resignation in his voice. Did he regret his decision? Was there something else? Despite herself, she felt a tingle of hope.

"We'll be in touch." Metatron turned on his heel and disappeared down the corridor with his entourage.

Kara stared after them in a cloud of cigar smoke.

She felt like someone had given her the moon.

She smiled wickedly.

CHAPTER 9
REVELATIONS

Mr. Patterson stared at Kara's face, his eyes wide with alarm.

"Dear souls! It is worse than I feared."

David, Peter, Jenny, and Ashley lingered behind Kara, but she could feel their fear for what was happening to her. The thought that they felt sorry for her made it worse. She didn't want anyone's pity. She just wanted to confirm her suspicions that she might have some kind of link with the knights and that the connection might enable her to break her dreaded curse.

If she was right.

"What does it mean?" Kara pulled her hood back over her head.

The oracle fumbled with his crystal ball nervously. "I'm not sure. It seems the mutation has progressed more rapidly than I had hoped. It's almost as though something *triggered* it."

Kara knew what had triggered it. She had.

"Do you think there's more to come?" David stepped in beside Kara.

He had taken the words right out of her mouth. But she could barely look at him for fear of what the oracle was about to say.

Mr. Patterson blinked the sadness from his eyes and looked back to Kara. "It's hard to say. Hold this."

He handed his crystal ball to David who took it carefully, surprised that the oracle trusted him to hold one of his precious crystals.

Then Mr. Patterson reached out and took her hand. He brushed his fingers over the black veins carefully, inspecting them. His fingers were soft and warm on her skin.

"Have more marks developed since the last outbreak? Since they last appeared on your face?"

The oracle inspected her hands closely. "Have you noticed if they keep progressing, is what I mean."

"I...I don't think so."

Kara stared at the bulging veins on her hands and tried not to make a face. They disgusted her. She disgusted herself.

"It's not like I'm keeping count, but they look the same. I mean, I don't think there's more. I think it stopped."

"Hmmm." Mr. Patterson watched her silently. "Or maybe just slowed down."

"Slowed down?" asked David, his brows furrowed. "So you don't think it's stopped yet?"

Mr. Patterson looked at Kara sadly. "We'll never know for sure. Not until we know precisely what these markings mean."

"Fantastic," growled David.

"But will Kara be okay?" Jenny's voice sounded from the back of the bookstore.

Jenny's face was drawn, and she gave Kara a tight smile that Kara found hard to return. Peter and Ashley were watching her, too. They looked worried that she might suddenly blow up or something.

Kara looked back at Mr. Patterson.

"I will speak to the oracle mothers about this," said the oracle with some urgency.

He let go of Kara's hand. "They are the wisest of our kind. They might have better answers for you. I wish…I wish we had more time. I could run some tests, maybe find a temporary remedy to slow the mutation…maybe even find a cure."

A cure.

"There's something I have to tell you. All of you." Kara waited until she had everyone's undivided attention. She had hoped that the oracle would have made the connection between her and the knights. But he hadn't. Now, she had no choice but to tell them what had happened.

Kara braced herself. "I think I have a theory about a cure."

"You never told me this?" said David with surprise.

"That's because I didn't know, well not for sure until I fought with the knight."

Mr. Patterson snatched his crystal back from David. "Go on."

They all gathered closer around her. "It's a working theory. I could be wrong—"

"But you think you're right." David's face was unreadable.

Kara's throat tightened. "When I injured the knight with my blade, I cut a deep wound into its left bicep. Well, it left a mark on me, too."

"What kind of a mark?" asked David quietly.

Kara kept her eyes on the oracle as she answered.

"A wound. Exactly like the one I left on the knight."

She watched as the oracle's eyes widened. She could see that his mind was working overtime. She could practically hear him think.

David raked his hair with his fingers. "What are you saying?"

"I'm saying that when I hurt the knight, *I* felt the pain, too. The cut. As soon as my blade perforated its skin—a gash opened up on *my* arm."

Mr. Patterson's face paled. "From what you are telling us, I fear you share a connection with these creatures. A physical connection."

Kara had suspected that she shared a connection with the knight, but hearing it confirmed by the oracle made it more likely to be true. She had been right. There *was* a connection.

Kara nodded. "I know. Well, at least that's what I thought. I'm linked to them somehow. The knight saw the wound on my arm, and it was just as surprised as I was. It wasn't expecting it either. So, for whatever reasons, I appear to be linked to the knights. But the fact that the knight didn't seem to know that I was linked to it in some way is even more confusing."

"So if you *are* linked to them," Ashley began, "couldn't you have warned us before it appeared? Didn't you *sense* it?"

"No. It doesn't work like that."

Kara didn't really know how it worked. It just did. She wasn't thrilled about it either. However, she hoped that her bond with the knights might provide her with a clue as to how she might rid herself of her mutation.

A shadow passed in the oracle's eyes.

"Kara, listen to me. I don't know what you are planning, but this…this dark supernatural energy is the worse there is. There is nothing more foul in all the worlds. The knights were forged from the archfiends' darkness and wickedness. Everything about them is evil. If you truly do share this connection, it could be very bad for you, and for the legion."

Kara was silent. She hadn't thought about that.

"I wish I could say that I'm not linked to them, but that would be a lie because I *felt* it. So how would this be bad for the legion exactly? I'm the one who's going through this, not them."

The more she thought carefully about the connection, the worse she felt. Had she made a mistake in telling everyone?

Mr. Patterson looked her in the face.

"Because, my dear, if *you* are linked to it…then it is also *linked* to you."

Kara felt like the oracle had slapped her. She bit her bottom lip. "I…I didn't think about that."

"Try not to fret, my dear. We'll make sense of this, I promise."

But Kara only felt worse. She wasn't sure what she had expected to hear, but that definitely wasn't part of it.

"You mean like it could read her mind or something?" inquired Jenny. "It could find out about the legion's secrets and plans. Everything."

Could Jenny be right?

Kara shivered at the thought of the knights rummaging through her mind, discovering her deepest secrets. Not just the legion's but her own. Could they sense what she was planning?

No.

She couldn't read their minds or sense them at all, so she was certain that they couldn't read her mind either. Whatever link they shared, it wasn't telepathic.

This conversation was not proceeding as Kara had planned. Jenny had not tried to anger her. She was just speaking her mind as she always did.

"I don't think it can read my mind," she said quietly to Jenny.

"Are you sure?" pressed Ashley, before Jenny could answer. "I mean, how would you know for sure?"

Kara's gaze shifted to Ashley. "Because I *can't* read their minds—"

"So they can't read *her* mind." David looked at Kara. "Makes sense."

"But that's if it works that way," said Ashley. "How can we know for sure? We can't, can we? Are we willing to take that chance? Kara...are you?"

Even though she didn't want to admit it, Kara knew that Ashley was right.

"Of course not. But what am I supposed to do? I still don't think they can read my mind. And if you *are* right, you still don't have much to worry about since the legion's never shared any secrets with me."

She couldn't help sounding bitter. "I don't know anything about any plans. There's not much in my head that can harm anyone, really. Just stupid stuff."

"Even so," began Mr. Patterson. "It would be wise if you didn't go back to Horizon. At least not until I speak with the oracle mothers. I believe it would be best for everyone."

Kara was taken aback.

Was that an order? She couldn't go back to Horizon? Was he afraid that she would infect the legion with her disease? Horizon was her home. She hadn't realized how much she cared about it until he suggested that she stay away. Even if it was just temporary...

The oracle was only trying to help her by telling her the truth. And she needed the truth. Besides, she needed to be here on Earth for her plan to work, and right now she needed to stick to her plan.

"Okay, I get it. I won't take any more risks with the legion. I'll stay here for as long as I can."

"I know this is difficult to hear, but it's for the best." Mr. Patterson brushed his crystal with his sleeve and then looked up at Kara, "And it won't be forever.

"I believe we went a little off track. So, what of your theory for a cure? What is it you think you know?"

At the mention of her theory, Kara's miserable thoughts about Horizon vanished.

"Like I said, it's just a theory…but I think it's going to work."

"Go on."

Kara was excited to continue.

"We know the archfiends are responsible for my changes. We still don't know why exactly, but we all know it's them. We also know that the archfiends created the knights. I think that I have some of whatever they used to create the knights in me. That would explain the bond I have with them. When I saw the wound on my arm after I stabbed the knight, I just knew. It became clear to me."

"What did?" David said.

"That I could kill it."

"But Kara—"

"The only way to get rid of my curse," Kara shuffled her wings, "is by getting rid of the archfiends."

She felt excited.

"It's a win-win for everyone. We destroy the knights, keep them from breaking the seals—the archfiends will go back to their cage and take their virus with them. The worlds will be saved, and I'll be back to normal again. I know it's going to work."

David and the others looked uneasy.

"What?" said Kara a little annoyed that they didn't jump for joy at her master plan. "Don't you want me to get better? Don't you want me to be normal again?"

"That's not it, Kara." David's eyes were filled with worry.

"Then what?"

"You said that when you cut the knight, it affected you too," said David.

"Yes. And?"

Kara concealed the flutter of irritation that surged through her. She wasn't sure if it was the darkness inside her, but her anger seemed to find her awfully quickly since her transformation. She had to fight to control it.

David tilted his head to the side.

"Doesn't that mean you might be at risk of killing yourself, if you kill any of the knights?"

"Yes," said Kara.

She saw that they all looked anxious. "And it's a risk I'm willing to take."

"It's not a risk *I'm* willing to take." David's expression toughened. "I won't risk your life."

"You don't have a choice." Kara's voice sounded harsher than she had intended.

"Look," she said softly as she recovered a little, "It's already in motion. The fate of the worlds depends on us. We need to succeed. I know what you're all thinking, and I've already thought it through long and hard. Yes, I might die...and I might *not*."

David clenched his jaw.

"I don't like this, Kara. It seems that every time something goes wrong...*you* always end up getting hit with the worst of it. It just doesn't seem fair. I just wish that I could take some of that burden, just this once, so you didn't have to."

The room went still.

Kara felt a cramp in her chest at David's concern for her. She wasn't embarrassed at his sudden revelation. She admired him and adored him all the more for it. If they had been alone, she would have kissed him hard and never let him go. But they weren't.

"I know, and truly I understand, believe me I do," she said. "I wish things could be different, but they're not. And I just have to accept them. I don't want to die my true death either, but I know within my soul that this is the right move. We'll finish what we started and move forward. Nothing's changed, well not that much. At least now we know that the knights can be killed."

"What makes you so sure?" inquired Peter. "You only stabbed it, and from what you just told us it wasn't a deadly cut. You said it yourself. You just injured it."

"Call it a hunch," said Kara. "If we can injure them, we can kill them."

"I have to agree with Kara, although it pains me to say it," said Jenny. "It's a relief, but also terrifying all at the same time," she continued softly.

Kara felt a lump in her throat.

"I'll be fine. Trust me. We'll hit these knights with whatever it takes. Don't hold back. You must promise me that."

She moved around them, watching their eyes.

"Promise me that you won't hold back, for my sake. Whatever it takes. Promise me."

Silence.

"Guys," pressed Kara. "I need you with me on this. I need your help, your skills as guardians. We're the best team in the legion—together. You know how important this is. It's more important than me. It's more important than all of us. It's the most important job we'll ever do. You must accept it, just as I accepted it."

"Fine, whatever it takes." David said a little reluctantly.

The others all agreed slowly, and Kara's excitement returned. They would destroy the knights, and she would be free.

Mr. Patterson paced. "Have you told anyone else about this?"

He turned to face Kara.

"No," she shook her head. "This is the first time I've spoken of it."

She wanted to add the fact that someone else had *seen* her markings, but she wasn't sure how to bring it up without putting the oracle in a state by revealing too much about her discussion with Metatron.

"Did anyone else see the marks on your face and hands when you were in Horizon?" asked the oracle. He might just as well have been reading her mind.

"Metatron saw me."

Mr. Patterson's fluffy white brows furrowed. "Why does that not surprise me?"

He turned away from her for a moment, as though trying to control himself.

He turned his attention back to Kara, his face contorted in rage. She had never seen him so angry.

"Did you speak to him?"

"Yes."

"What did he tell you?"

After sighing loudly, Kara recounted the events that had occurred between her and the archangel. He had seen the marks and her wings. She had told him about the attack on the archfiends and she almost tipped him off about their plans. She told Mr. Patterson everything except the part about the deal. No one needed to know about that.

"I apologize for not mentioning that this mission was not an *official* one," began the oracle.

He turned the crystal orb in his hand anxiously.

"I was afraid that you all might not want to take it. And that was a not chance that the oracle mothers and I were willing to take. There is too much at stake, and we had to bend the rules a little."

"Don't worry about it, Mr. P," said Jenny grinning. "We love anything *unofficial*."

David smiled. "Yeah, we would have agreed to it anyway. All of us."

"Yeah," agreed Ashley and Peter in unison.

The oracle beamed at their confidence in him.

"It's fine," said Kara, "but I almost gave us away. In fact, I'm pretty sure Metatron will figure it out sooner or later. He was *really* angry."

"Yes," said Mr. Patterson, a mischievous smiled played on his lips. "I bet he was."

Kara shared a sidelong glance with David.

"Did something happen between you and Metatron?" asked Kara.

The idea that the oracle might derive some pleasure out of angering the archangel was too sweet to pass. She wanted to know a little more about the newly appointed commander. Maybe she could learn something that she could use against him to trade with if he ever tried to make a deal with her again.

Mr. Patterson dismissed her with a wave of his hand.

"That is a story for another day. And don't worry about Metatron. I'll deal with him when the time comes. Now, you best hurry. We don't have much time left to stop the knights. It's our only chance."

"Where do we begin our search?" asked Peter, although his voice was void of enthusiasm.

"Boston," answered David. Kara raised her brows in surprise.

"I was talking with the archangel Raphael, and she hinted to me that a whole plague of diseases originated in Boston."

"Well, it's a start," said Kara.

She wondered if the archangel had intended to reveal so much to David. *Did the archangel know of their secret mission?* Her angel intuition told her that this wasn't a coincidence. Raphael knew where one of the knights was, and she had just told David where to look.

"It sounds like this could be the handiwork of the knight called Pestilence, right?"

Mr. Patterson gave her a small nod of his head. "If Raphael mentioned it to David, then it's definitely worth a look."

As they took their leave, Kara couldn't help but notice the nervous glances everyone kept giving her as they stepped onto the street. *Did they think she couldn't see them?*

The news of Kara's link to the knights had put a damper on the excitement they would normally have felt at going on a secret mission. The quest was different this time. It was complicated.

Mr. Patterson stood sadly at his front door and watched them leave. Her friends' long faces caused a wrench in her chest, but there was no room for gloom or regret now.

Kara felt excited and determined. Her mind was active, and she whispered the same word to herself over and over again.

Normal.

CHAPTER 10
BOSTON, MASSACHUSETTS

Kara and the others were silent as they walked along Fruit
Street and made their way toward the Boston, Massachusetts
General Hospital.

Kara took comfort from the thought that the archangel
Raphael might be on their side, but it wasn't enough. The
knowledge that the legion had ordered a strike for tomorrow left
the team sullen and on edge. They all had friends in the legion who
wouldn't survive, no matter how many legions of angels and
archangels fought, or how resilient they thought they were. It didn't
matter how many demon legions fought with them. The archfiends
were stronger.

Kara had caught a glimpse of a local newspaper as they strolled
down the street. Crops and livestock all over the world had
suddenly dried up, rotted, and withered away. The mortals were

117

blaming global warming and a short winter. But there was no scientific explanation for the millions of carcasses.

The angels knew better. This was only the beginning.

Kara's icy cold fear that she would die if she killed one of the knights never left her. She had told everyone that she accepted her fate, no matter what. She had a reputation to uphold. But deep down, Kara was terrified.

She didn't want to die her true death. She wanted to *live*. It didn't matter whether she survived as a guardian or a mortal, as long as it was a life with David. It was beginning to feel like a fantasy.

She continued to struggle with the darkness inside her. Now that she had unleashed it, she felt it slowly spreading, and she feared she could no longer control it. It might be foolish, but she still had hope. The part of her that was angel still believed she could change the course of the future—she would not become the monster that killed her friends.

But the darkness inside her was intoxicating. She had power that went beyond anything she had ever felt, even beyond her elemental powers. It was *addictive*. And like an addict, she trembled in cold sweats as she fought the urge to succumb completely, to lose herself.

And so she walked in silence and clenched her fists in the attempt to keep the darkness at bay. She had to restrain it until she met another knight.

As soon as they arrived at the hospital, Kara knew something was very wrong.

Masses of people lay on the road in front of the red brick building. Their faces were covered in boils, blood, and sores. They looked like someone had taken a cheese grater to them. Their clothes were splattered and drenched in maroon stains. Kara saw a young man vomiting blood, and she winced when he collapsed on a pile of infected bodies. Mothers cried tears of blood as they clutched their dead babies. People's bodies and faces were encrusted with sores that looked like third degree burns. Moaning and wailing filled the air around them like a symphony from hell. It reminded Kara of a scene from a zombie movie. Everyone was infected.

Kara moved carefully through the dead and infected, careful not to step on anyone or on anyone's severed limbs. She covered her nose, but it was impossible not to smell it. It was everywhere, in the air and on their clothes. They stood paralyzed by the horror of it all.

And as she looked at the sick and the dead, Kara became mesmerized by all the blood. It drew her in and nourished that part of her soul that was corrupted. Part of her enjoyed the scene, enjoyed watching the suffering. The stench became a luring fragrance. Darkness clouded her mind, and she forgot why she was here. An intoxicating wickedness spread across her chest, down her arms and legs, and into her wings.

She heard her friends' voices and clung to the knowledge of their friendship to regain control. Her body trembled as she overcame the evil that had been triggered by the sight of all the dead bodies. She clenched her jaw and pushed the darkness down.

She turned her head away to help clear her mind. But everywhere she looked, the dead plagued her vision, their arms reaching out in a last desperate attempt to reach the hospital. This was no natural disease. This was supernatural evil, and only the supernatural could defeat it.

She was overcome with a cold anger, an anger to kill.

"Are you feeling okay?" David appeared by her side. "You're shaking."

Kara could feel his fear. She knew that when they found the knight, David would be afraid to strike in case he hurt her in the process. She knew him too well. But they had no choice. *She* had no choice. They would have to try.

"I'm fine," she lied. She was disgusted with herself for the brief moment of satisfaction she had felt at the sight of the dead.

"All these people. All these sick people. It's a lot to take in."

She hated herself.

"It is," said David. "You think the knight's still here?"

"I do," she said, shaking her head. "I don't feel its *presence* or anything like that, but I know it's here. Probably gloating at all the sickness and death it spread."

"Like some serial killers that come back to the scene of the crime," said Jenny.

"They like to relive the crime."

"It's sick," said Peter coldly.

"This isn't your typical serial killer, either." Ashley moved slowly among the dead, inspecting them more closely, like she thought she might actually be able to help them.

"I wish we could help them." Jenny looked like she was about to break down. "We *have* to do something. Maybe we can find a cure or something? Or maybe find something to help relieve the pain?"

"There's nothing we can do for them," said Peter gently. "There's no cure, Jenny. These are not normal diseases."

He was silent for a moment. "If you want to help them, then we have to find a way to keep the seals from breaking. It's the only way."

Jenny shook her head, her bottom lip quivered. "But that's like—how many more people are going to die before we stop the knights? Thousands? Millions?"

"More than we can imagine," whispered Ashley.

Jenny nocked an arrow angrily. "I'm going to kill them. I *swear* I will."

"That's the idea." Ashley swung her sword over her head and stood in a fighting stance. Her smile grew wider.

While Kara appreciated Jenny and Ashley's courage and was grateful to have them by her side, she knew that arrows and swords wouldn't be enough to defeat the knights.

Suddenly, Kara felt a cold presence.

She scanned the scene and saw it immediately. On the flat roof of the hospital she could see the silhouette of a specter sitting on a giant steed. Even from a distance she could tell it was watching *her*. It sat calmly, waiting, waiting for Kara.

"It's up there." Kara pointed with her blade to the rooftop. And before anyone could stop her, she spread her wings and soared into the sky.

"Kara! Wait! It's too dangerous!" she heard David cry out.

"We don't know what'll happen to you!"

But she ignored him and beat her great black wings. She wanted to kill it herself.

She hated the knight, and she hated herself. She let her hatred control and fuel her. She didn't want to think about what would happen to her. Nothing mattered anymore.

She landed on the hospital roof and folded her wings.

Like its brethren, the knight was enormous. But unlike Famine, Pestilence wasn't bony thin and haggard but thick with rippling diseased muscles. Beneath a metal armor, its skin was wet. It was covered in festering boils, rashes, and growths, like it carried every possible disease on itself. It was its own plague. She could see its red eyes watching her from behind its metal helmet, and it held two great swords in its giant hands. The knight was mounted on a tawny colored horse, and like its master the beast's coat was infected by disease. Kara winced at the rank smell that rolled off of them. It was the stench of a million dead corpses rotting in the sun.

She kept her distance and tried very hard to hide the fear she felt inside. She watched the knight and waited for an opportunity to draw her blade quickly. The only target she could see was the head. If she could slip her blade into its eye, she might be able to stab its brain. *Would that kill it? Could she kill it? Would she kill herself?*

Her friends would be running up the stairs and bursting out onto the roof any minute now. She had to kill it before they arrived. She had to do something. She clenched her dagger so tightly that her fingers ached. There was only one way to find out.

There was no time to think or figure out plots. There was only time to attack.

The darkness pulsed inside her, and in that instant she knew she had to use it.

Like an assassin, she sprang with only death on her mind.

With a single, great flap of her wings, Kara shot like a missile toward the knight with her dagger aimed at the creature's head.

The knight sneered. Its black pointed teeth looked like spikes.

Just as the tip of her blade was inches from the creature's eyes, a shadow passed in front of her eyes, and something hard punched her in the chest. Kara went spiraling through the air and crashed on the rooftop. But she was up on her feet again in an instant and attacked the knight again.

Some kind of steam drifted from its helmet. Its scarlet eyes glowed, and its diseased face showed a smile. But Kara didn't have time to dwell on how ugly this beast was, she sought only to kill it.

She leaped from the roof, and with a roar of rage, she flew at him again.

The knight swung one of his great swords and caught Kara in the chest. Pain exploded inside her, and she landed on her side on the roof. Ignoring the pain, she rolled over and leapt to her feet. Her wings beat behind her wildly and echoed the fury that surged through her. She turned and faced her opponent again.

The knight howled in delight, and his voice boomed above the rooftop like the crackling of thunder.

"Give up, child of darkness. Why do you oppose us? Why do you fight what you are?"

Kara spit the dirt from her mouth.

"I don't know what you mean and frankly I *don't* care. I fight for what's right. I fight for the fate of the mortals. I fight for the angels."

"The angels?" The knight's sneer expanded and his shoulders shook in silent laughter. Sores on its shoulders burst and festering rivulets of orange pus seeped out of the blisters and over its metal armor like hot wax.

Kara turned her face away in disgust. The way its sores burst open whenever it moved, and its overpowering smell of sickness and death repulsed her even more than the first knight.

The knight circled Kara. The steed was graceful and light on its feet for a creature that was diseased. Kara stayed still.

The knight's voice echoed in the air again.

"The fight between angels and man is over. The time for the dark gods is now. It is too late…too late for this world…too late for the other worlds. Our dark gods will make a dominion of darkness. Night and decay and death will hold dominion over all. Death is inevitable. The legion was bound to fail from the beginning. There is no hope for mortals. It is over."

"There's always hope."

The knight snickered. "I feel the darkness in you. The shadow world is strong inside you. You will become great. Soon you will not care about these humans or this world, and you will join us."

"Never."

"You know I speak the truth. You can feel it inside, can't you? The cold power calls to you, and you have already set it free. Embrace what you are to become. Embrace what you are. Embrace the darkness."

"I'm going to cut out your tongue if you don't shut up...that's if you even *have* one."

"The angels and all ethereal creatures that do not surrender and bow to the true dark gods will perish."

Kara didn't want to hear words anymore.

But somewhere deep inside her soul, she knew it was right. Her mutation was nearly finished, and she could feel the cold power flourishing inside as though it belonged in her. She was meant to be on the wrong side, the side that killed innocents. That killed angels.

"It's too late now. You know I speak the truth. Soon *you* will join the darkness."

Her memories from the white oracle still haunted her. Kara screamed in rage. She hit her head repeatedly with the pommel of her dagger.

"I won't. I'm not evil!" she cried. "I'm an *angel.*"

"You are no longer an angel."

"SHUT UP!"

Kara's hatred throbbed with a cold, dull ache, and she felt the cool, untamed power ripple down her spine and spread to her wings. It clouded her mind with thoughts of death. The dead, whispered in her ears, coercing her, compelling her to believe that all those who had died would have died anyway. She would be showing them no mercy. Kill them all.

"No, I don't want this."

She shook her head and whimpered at the desperation she felt as she tried to maintain control.

The darkness had lied to her. It was trying to trick her. She *had* to make it stop. She had to stop the knights. Her head cleared momentarily, and she focused all her malice on the repulsive knight. She wanted to shut it up, to stop it from speaking the dreaded truth she already knew.

"I am an angel," she wailed, partly to the monster and partly to herself.

In a wild fury, Kara threw her blade. As she watched the blade lance across the rooftop, she knew it wouldn't kill the knight, but it certainly would anger it. Maybe it would anger it enough that it would dismount, and then maybe she'd have a fighting chance. The blade flew straight and true and sank deep into the knight's neck in the unprotected part near the clavicles.

The knight thrashed about in sudden surprise and pain, but Kara staggered, too, as a searing pain burned a spot on her own neck in the exact same place where she had hit the knight. She pressed on her wound with her hand and looked up.

A mix of black and orange pus spurted from around the blade where it had hit the knight. She might have hit an artery. The steed neighed and reared up on its back legs, but the knight stayed on. He pulled out her blade and tossed it at her feet, challenging her to try again. It was nothing to him.

Kara absorbed all of her pain and anger and fury and let it fill every inch of her. Then she picked up her blade, screamed, and threw herself toward the knight like a bullet.

The knight sneered and flicked his hand. The shadows rose up again and slammed Kara to the ground. She fell, rolled, and tried to get on her feet, but another shadow wrapped itself around her waist and yanked her sideways. The knight flicked his wrist again, and Kara was lifted and hurled back onto the rooftop. The impact crushed her wings, and she lay in a heap on the ground.

As tendrils of black shadow cut through Kara's skin and made furrows in her flesh, her screams grew louder.

Another shadow tightened around her ankle, and she groaned as it lifted her off the ground. She dangled upside down, swaying, trying to breathe. White light exploded behind her eyes, and then the shadows vanished.

"Stay down, if you know what's good for you. I don't want to destroy you, but I will if you do not cooperate."

Kara screamed in rage. She snarled. And then she was back on her feet, running as fast as she could toward the knight, her wings dangling behind her like useless baggage. She lunged and smashed into the steed.

The blunt force of the impact threw the creature sideways, and it stumbled. The knight slipped off his ride and crashed to the floor.

Kara was on top of the knight in seconds. Just its smell was enough to knock her out, but she threw herself at it wildly and hit it over and over again in its unprotected face.

More shadows sent Kara sprawling, but she clambered to her feet and threw herself at the knight again.

The creature raised its arms, ready to shoot out more shadow tendrils, but Kara was faster.

With incredible speed she dodged, spun, and hurled herself at the knight's head again. She thrust her blade into any unprotected space she could find around its neck and face, slicing, stabbing, and cutting, over and over. She cried in fury and in pain as she desperately attempted to kill it. She didn't care if she killed herself in the process.

Pain exploded in her head, and Kara was thrown in the air again.

She landed with an agonizing crack, but she ignored the deep wounds and the searing pain in her own face and neck, staggered to her feet, and faced the knight.

More orange and black blood oozed from deep gashes in the knight's face and neck, and as he advanced, he staggered. It was hardly noticeable, just a slight pause, but Kara noticed. She had injured it, which meant she *could* kill it.

"You think you can destroy me?" laughed the creature. "You think by destroying me you can stop your transformation? I know what you are…and what you'll become. You cannot stop what is inevitable. The final stages of your transformation have commenced. You are no longer an angel. Accept it. Embrace your fate."

With her blade still clasped tightly in her hand, Kara screamed in fury and ran.

But she hadn't taken more than three steps when something crashed into her from the side, and she went tumbling. Her head hit the ground hard, and she heard a crunch. Her chin scraped the metal roof, and she skidded to a stop. For half a second she lay there, dazed. Her head throbbed. She could barely think. *What had happened? Had the knight's horse kicked her?*

When she rolled over and pushed herself back to her feet, she thought for sure that she must still have been stunned from her head injury because she stared straight into the identical faces of three higher demons.

CHAPTER 11
CONVICTED

Kara cursed under her breath and then turned on the demons. "Are you stupid? What are you doing?" she hissed.

A higher demon raised his eyebrows with an evil sneer on his pasty face. "Saving you, of course."

"Saving me?" Kara staggered forward. Her head throbbed more than ever as the pain from her injuries finally reached her and ploughed through her body like a hundred death blades stabbing her at once. She could hardly stand. *Did she just hear them laugh?* She blinked the black spots from her eyes.

"I don't need saving, you fools!"

The higher demons looked amused. Their pallid faces and cruel black eyes stared at her coldly.

She pushed past the higher demons. "Get out of my way. Move I said! I've got him. I can kill him. I've got the knight—"

But she stumbled when she saw that the knight and his steed were gone.

A few speckles of orange and black liquid were the only signs that the knight had existed at all. He was gone. She had failed.

At that moment a door on the roof exploded open and David, Peter, Jenny, and Ashley rushed onto the roof.

"Where's the knight?" David eyed the higher demons that stood sneering at them.

"Where is he? Kara?"

Kara looked to the last spot where she had seen the creature. She felt warm liquid roll down her face and neck. It trickled down her arm until it dripped from the tip of her blade. She blanched. It was not the brilliant white essence of an angel, but the black blood of a demon.

"Kara, what happened here?" David came up by her side.

"You look like you took a beating. I hope the knight looks as thrashed as you do."

He paused and then he added excitedly. "That's it. You got him, didn't you? You killed the knight!" He sounded so pleased and proud of her that she felt even worse.

"What? Did you really destroy it, Kara? How did you do it?" Jenny sounded elated.

But Kara couldn't look at them. She could barely hear them all. All she heard were the words from the knight. They echoed in her mind as she stared at her black blood.

You are no longer an angel.

"What's wrong with her?" Ashley walked slowly around Kara and then faced her.

"She looks...a little *off*." Her eyes widened. "And she's bleeding. She's bleeding *black* blood."

So now they all knew. Kara opened her mouth, but the words would not come.

"Kara?" David slipped his hand in Kara's free hand and squeezed it gently.

"You're hurt. What happened here?" he asked tenderly.

When she didn't answer, he turned from her and eyed the demons.

"And *why* are you three douchebag demons here? And why do I get the feeling you're to blame for her injuries, eh? What did you do to her?"

"We did nothing to the female," said one of the higher demons smoothly. He sounded innocent, but Kara felt the deceitful undertones.

"We were ordered to come here. That is all. We were ordered to help."

"That's right," said another higher demon, "we were charged to help you."

"Help? Why?" David glowered. "We never asked for *your* help. How did you even know we were here? Did you follow us?"

The three higher demons watched David, but didn't answer.

"Kara," said Peter as he made his way over to her. "Did you kill it? Did you vanquish one of the knights?"

Kara raised her eyes to Peter, but still she couldn't find her voice.

"Everybody, check your rings," said Jenny suddenly. She wiggled her fingers. "I still got mine—"

"My ring's gone," said David. Everyone looked at his bare hand. "We were too late. Another seal is broken."

Jenny looked at Kara thoughtfully. "So you *didn't* defeat it. It defeated you. It defeated us. This bites."

"It seems that luck is *not* on our side," said Ashley as she circled the higher demons with her sword in her hand. "We've only got two seals left. These odds suck."

"At this rate, it doesn't look like we're going to make it." Jenny shook her head. "And from what Mr. P said I get the feeling that the last two knights are the worst. How are we going to beat them?"

"We're not going to make it," said Ashley gloomily. "It's over."

"Don't say that," said Peter. "It's not over, there's *still* a chance," but the quiver in his voice betrayed him.

But when he spoke next, his voice was full of valor, as though it had been there a long time and had suddenly awoken.

"We still have time, there's a little more than two days left. We can still defeat the remaining two. I have to believe. No. We *must* believe we can do it. If we don't have faith, then this mission has already failed. The fates of the worlds depend on us succeeding. There's no room for failure."

"I hear ya, Pete," said David. "But I hate to burst your bubble. I have to agree with Ashley on this one. These things keep slipping away from us and time's running out. They've got superpowers from the dark gods, and all we've got are these…"

He waved his soul blade.

"If Kara had defeated this one, then maybe we would have been on the winning side. As of now, we're on the loser's team."

Kara had heard enough.

"*They* did this," she snarled as she eyed the higher demons and gripped her soul blade in her bloodied hand.

Jenny watched Kara carefully. "Who did what, exactly?"

Kara let go of David's hand. "I had him. I was going to kill him. But they…" her eyes met the three higher demons, and she scowled wildly. "They stopped me."

Kara looked into those black, soulless eyes, and she knew they had stopped her on purpose. The demons had *saved* the knight from her wrath. The demons had seen that she had had an opening and was about to kill the knight. They had sensed that she might even survive.

Kara knew that the demons had their own agenda. She didn't know exactly what it was—yet—but she would find out.

For now, all she knew for certain was that they had stopped her from killing the knight, and in the process they had ruined their chances of stopping the apocalypse.

Her chances to become normal again were disappearing.

"They stopped me from killing it on *purpose*," she hissed.

She moved slowly toward the demons, like a predator about to kill its prey. Her throbbing headache had gone, and it had been replaced by a pulsing hatred for the demons.

"Are you freaking kidding me?" David waved his blade menacingly toward the demons, but Kara was already there.

She raised her blade and roared like an animal. There was nothing angelic about her behavior. She was projecting all her hatred for taking away her chance of becoming a normal angel again upon the demons. She heard the shouts of her friends, but she ignored them as she lunged for the higher demons.

The higher demons hissed and snarled as they sprang at Kara with their death blades.

Kara dove into the demons with a fountain of savage, unforgiving cold power. She could smell, hear, and see everything with heightened senses that gave her an advantage over the demons, over everything.

"Kara, you can't do this!" she heard David's cry over the pounding of power in her ears.

"Don't do this! There's a treaty! They won't forgive you this time!"

But Kara paid no attention. Kara would never have fought or wanted to fight three higher demons at the same time when she only had elemental power. But things were different now, *she* was different, and she bellowed her challenge.

The higher demons answered her challenge. They rushed at her in a blur of gray. Their death blades glistened in the dull light as they attacked. She ran at them, flinging her blade and slashing at them with cold power.

They dodged and blocked her every blow, hissing and grunting at her triumphantly as though they had already won. Kara knew that they were mocking her because she had seen through their lies. She knew that they had helped the knight escape from her grasp.

She halted. Her soul blade was too weak. The demons smiled confidently.

She tossed the blade on the ground and called forth all her cold, raw power. The demons tensed, as though they sensed what she was about to do. But it was already too late for them.

Kara embraced her darkness. Enraged, she spun in the air and decapitated them all with a powerful swing of her giant razor blade wings. She landed on the ground next to their headless bodies, and their heads rolled to her feet.

Their bodies and heads disintegrated into black dust and disappeared in a gust of wind.

"Kara, what have you done?"

Kara froze.

She recognized that voice. It didn't belong to any of her friends. Bracing herself, she turned around slowly and met the archangel Ariel's fierce stare.

CHAPTER 12
FUGITIVE

"What is the meaning of this?"

The authority of the archangel Ariel's voice cut through Kara's dark madness.

What was the archangel doing here?

Kara wanted to shy away when she saw the look of horror that flashed momentarily in the archangel's eyes. It was gone just as fast as it had appeared, but it lasted long enough for Kara to have felt it.

"My. My. My." Metatron stepped from behind Ariel, and Kara flinched. His angel entourage all had blades in their hands, and they all watched Kara with loathing.

"She killed *three* higher demons with her wings. Remarkable," said Metatron, although there was nothing commendable in his tone.

Ariel frowned and examined Kara carefully.

"Why? Why would you do this when you knew we had an accord with the demons? We have a treaty. We need them. If we're to beat the archfiends, we need to collaborate with the demon legions. How could you do this, Kara?"

Kara suspected that the archangel wanted an apology rather than an explanation.

But she wasn't sorry at all. She knew the truth. The treaty was a joke to the demons. They didn't believe in it, so why should she? David looked shocked, but she could see that he feared what was going to happen to her.

"If word reaches the demons about this…about what you've done," said Ariel, her beautiful features twisted in a deep scowl, "there'll be repercussions."

"They'll take it as a threat and as grounds for retaliation." Metatron made his way to Kara.

"What you just did is a serious violation of our treaty with them. We can't afford to lose the demons now, not when we face the biggest battle of our time. Yes, they're slimly and ugly and they smell of death, but by gods they can fight. We need them."

"Was it those markings on your face?" asked Ariel. "Was it the mutation that made you do this? Where you compelled in some way?" There was a trace of hope in Ariel's voice. She hoped that Kara wasn't a murderer.

But it wasn't the case.

Kara knew that everyone, even David, thought the exact same thing. She had to clear the air.

"No," she said, her anger still rippled on her lips.

Even though the higher demons were gone, their foul stink lingered in the air and reminded her of their treachery.

She looked at Metatron. "They didn't respect your *treaty*. They're not loyal to us, to the legion. I know they have another agenda. I had a clear shot. I had an opening to kill Pestilence, one of the four knights of the apocalypse. And just when I was about to finish him off, they *stopped* me. They came out of nowhere and pushed me down. And when I got back on my feet the knight was gone."

Ariel gave her a bemused look and then crossed her arms. "Is that what really happened?"

"Yes. I swear it."

Metatron watched her with barely concealed surprise. Clearly, he didn't believe a word that came out of her mouth.

"Can anyone else corroborate her story?" he inquired. "Did anyone else see this? Because all we saw was her assassinate three higher demons."

Kara's team stared at one another. Jenny paled. She eyed Peter, who adjusted his glasses nervously. Ashley was stony faced, but her knitted brows showed that she was fighting with something internally.

David had kept his eyes on Metatron.

After a few seconds of silence he said, "I did. They stopped her just as she was about to kill the knight. I was there. I saw it all. What Kara's telling you is the truth."

It took every ounce of Kara's power to keep a straight face. David lied so effortlessly. She was shocked.

Metatron looked at him for a very long moment. "And you'd be willing to swear on the souls that this is true?" He grinned with an odd twisted expression.

David's eyes flashed. "I would!"

Metatron surveyed David from under his shades. He smiled slightly and twisted his cigar in his hands. "You're lying, boy."

"I'm not."

"Don't embarrass yourself any further, Mr. McGowan. I can always tell when someone is lying. That's just one of my many talents. You don't want to get on my bad side, Davy. That is *my* truth."

The air above Metatron darkened as though a storm was brewing.

Rage started to fill Kara again, and she shifted on her feet. She turned to Metatron and gazed up into his smug, oily face.

"Leave David out of this," she said.

Everyone looked at her.

"I killed the demons. You saw it. Everyone saw that part. But what you didn't see, and what I'm telling you, is *my* truth. The demons made sure I couldn't touch the knight. They jeopardized our mission. David has done nothing wrong. If you're so good at spotting a lie, then surely you can spot the truth."

Metatron grinned evilly and pointed his cigar at her.

"But that's where you're wrong. You are lying because there is *no* mission here. You're all on an unauthorized mission. You shouldn't even be here. We shouldn't be here. You're all in violation

140

of the Angel Code. And if we didn't need you tomorrow, you'd all be locked up in Tartarus for insubordination."

"What!" Jenny was outraged. "You can't do that!"

David stepped dangerously close to Metatron, who, although he wasn't as tall as Ariel, was still much taller and broader than David.

"What the heck are you talking about?" David did his best to look surprised.

Metatron took a drag of his cigar and blew it in David's face.

"Like I said, there is *no* official mission here. And all of you," he pointed to each guardian with his cigar, "are in violation of the Code. I've killed guardians for lesser crimes than this. You can look at it however you want, but the bottom line is that this is a crime."

"Hey, just a second," Ashley raised her hands. "Let's not get ahead of ourselves. Clearly there's been a misunderstanding."

David barked out a laugh. "This is crazy."

"No, not crazy," said Metatron. "According to the legion, and your boss—" he turned and looked at Ariel. "The five of you have abandoned your posts."

Kara glared at Metatron.

His smile widened. In some sick way he enjoyed watching her get angry. There was no point in lying anymore. He knew.

"The oracle lied." Metatron blew a sphere of smoke out of his mouth and then poked a hole in it with his finger.

"Yes, your beloved Mr. Patterson took it upon himself to send you on an unauthorized and dangerous mission. There is no mission. There never was."

141

He raised his brows. "I knew you were hiding something when I saw you lurking in the shadows. I know when someone's hiding something from me. That's when I *knew* the oracle you call Mr. Patterson was involved. I knew he had sent his *favorite* on this ridiculous quest."

Kara felt a jolt of tension. Her anger simmered, barely in control.

She cared deeply for Mr. Patterson. She loved him. Having anyone destroy his good name was like a kick in the face. She had never liked Metatron, but now her animosity toward him was more like deep loathing. She wanted to punch that smug face more than ever. The world around her disappeared and only she and Metatron remained. Where was that dagger of hers?

"Oracles fill the heads of angels with tall tales, myths, legends…their fables are legendary," said Metatron. "Unfortunately, they do have their uses. But I think this Mr. Patterson has been stationed on earth too long. Clearly it's affected his mind. It wasn't his place to give out missions, especially ones that are destined to fail."

Kara shared a look with David, but he kept his face blank.

"Mr. Patterson's been challenging me and my methods for centuries, a lot longer than you've known him," continued Metatron. "I've always had trouble with that oracle…always stirring up nonsense, spreading fear. He already came to us with this ridiculous scheme about the four knights and seals."

He waved his arms in the air. "All of it a fabrication, a figment of the oracle's imagination. There is no proof or guarantee that any of it would work, and so he was turned down and ordered to keep his big mouth shut and to forget his master plan."

Metatron frowned. "But I see now, that he didn't."

"The guardians aren't to blame," voiced Ariel. "They thought they were acting on orders from us, from me, which isn't true. They would have never sought out this mission if they'd known it wasn't authorized."

Kara and the others kept their faces blank. She had to remember to commend them for such great acting. It was the only thing to keep them from Tartarus. If Ariel knew the truth, there was no way of telling what would happen to them.

"They're my best team, and I see no reason to pursue this any further. I need them back, Metatron."

Metatron smiled lazily at Ariel.

"Sure. These four, you can have back. I don't care." He turned on Kara. "But this one. This one almost ruined *everything*. This one's mine."

Kara's rage took her to a place where she only knew three things: that she was a weapon forged to end lives, that if she went to Tartarus the archfiends would win, and that her hopes of becoming a normal angel were being crushed.

She didn't care what sort of information they expected to twist from her. She wasn't a traitor. They could torture her for all eternity. She didn't care because she did not intend to let them take her.

Metatron turned his head and addressed his girls. "Take her prisoner. And when I've finished with her, once and for all, we'll see what finally bleeds out of her."

"You can't do this!"

David moved and shielded Kara with his body. Kara felt tenderness for his loyalty. But this wasn't the time to be brave.

Metatron smiled smoothly. "Oh, but I can and I will."

He cleared his throat. "Kara Nightingale, you are under arrest for a violation of the Angel treaty with the Netherworld, and for the murder of three higher demons. You are to be sentenced to Tartarus for an undefined term."

"Ariel, do something!" cried David. "You can't let him do this. This is crazy. You know Kara. You know she's not a liar. The higher demons betrayed us. They're not on our side."

Ariel's face was full of sorrow. "I'm sorry, David. There's nothing to support her story. There's nothing I can do. She broke the laws. I'm sorry."

The archangel avoided Kara's eyes. Peter and Ashley both looked like they were about to break down, and Jenny swayed unsteadily like she might pass out.

David turned to Metatron.

"I won't let you do this. I won't."

Metatron shook his head. "Davy, Davy, Davy. If you try and stop me, then I'll have no choice but to throw you in Tartarus with her. But in separate cells, of course."

"Do it then," barked David.

Even though Kara was overwhelmed by David's affection for her and for the sacrifice he was willing to make, she couldn't let him do this. She would never let him suffer for her.

Kara pushed David aside and turned to him. "I can't let you do this."

His eyes traced the black lines over her face. "I won't let them take you away from me."

Kara pressed her lips firmly together to keep them from trembling. And then she said softly. "They won't."

Kara knew what she needed to do. There was the only way to keep everyone safe.

And before anyone could react, she pushed off hard with her wings and soared in the air.

They called after her, but she didn't look down. When she'd decided she'd ascended high enough, she glanced down at Metatron and his groupies below.

The women flashed their blades and pointed in Kara's direction, like they were about to shoot them at her, like darts.

Metatron looked like a tiny rat from where Kara was, and she couldn't help but smile.

"Don't!" he growled.

Even from a distance she couldn't mistake his glare through his shades.

"If you go, there's no coming back. You're assuring your own death sentence."

"I'm already dead," called Kara.

She winced at the pain she saw in in David's eyes. She turned away. If she looked at him again, she might actually decide to stay. But she couldn't. She wouldn't.

"What's the point now?" she hissed and flapped her wings savagely.

"Look at me! Look at what I've become. Look at what the archfiends did to me. I'm not even an angel anymore. I'm just a thing, a dark corrupted thing."

"Don't," warned Metatron. "I won't tell you again."

The groupies raised their weapons and smiled at the chance to hurt her. They wanted to see her squirm in pain. Metatron's groupies were much more like him than she had first thought. They wanted to inflict pain, and they were going to *like* it.

Kara stared down at the stunned faces of her friends. David gave a slight nod of his head.

It was all she needed.

"Shoot her down!" ordered Metatron.

His groupies' blades flew like spears into the sky toward Kara.

She did the only thing she could.

With a great push of her wings, Kara climbed higher into the air and disappeared in the dark gray sky.

CHAPTER 13

FRIENDS AND FOES

Only one blade nicked her thigh, and she didn't even notice it until later when she felt something wet roll down her leg.

She flew above the clouds. The two-hour journey from Boston to Mr. Patterson's bookstore was nearing its end, and she hoped to get there before Metatron's cronies. She didn't want to imagine what they'd do to the old man. She banked slowly and tucked in her wings a little as she began her descent.

What would she do if she came face to face with Metatron? The thought that his ugly face would be twisted in fury made Kara smile. She'd enjoyed seeing him squirm.

The lights of the city gleamed like stars, and her chest tightened as her thoughts moved to David. She remembered the last night they'd been on a date together. The night lights had lit up his eyes, and she remembered how desperately handsome he was and how she wanted to kiss him.

Would she ever get to have a normal life again with David? Would the end of the world come too soon?

Hopefully Metatron wouldn't take his revenge out on David. But Metatron was such a loose cannon of an archangel, who knew what would happen to David. Hopefully Ariel would knock some sense into the legion's commander. Hopefully. But even if Metatron pardoned David and the others, they would be ordered to fight the archfiends in a few hours anyway. The thought of the legion fighting alongside the black-eyed demons sent a wave of fury through Kara. The demons weren't in alliance with anyone but themselves. Ice in her gut spread into her black veins. Somehow she would prove to everyone just how treacherous the demons were.

She had gotten but a taste of the archfiend's power when she fought the knights. *What other creatures had the archfiends created? How much more powerful were they now that two seals had been broken?*

Kara knew that Mr. Patterson's so-called *unauthorized* mission was still the right thing to do. She had faith in the old man, and she suspected that the archangel Raphael did, too.

She knew what she had to do. She was going after the third knight on her own.

As she flew toward Montreal, she brushed her hand over the places on her neck and shoulder where she had been wounded. She let out a little startled gasp. Her wounds were gone. Her skin had healed.

Kara wasn't all that surprised. She felt different. Her skin felt different. It was almost as though her M-suit had shredded away like snakeskin. Her new skin didn't need to replenish itself. She wouldn't need to go to Horizon to replenish her strength because her wounds healed themselves. And she felt stronger than ever.

She suspected she could never return to Horizon again, not because she had escaped, but because of what she felt she was *becoming*. The monster that brewed inside her was not angel, but something else, something darker, something much more sinister. She tasted it. She felt it. It was inside her, and it was cold and dark. There wasn't time to feel sorry for herself. It didn't matter anymore. What mattered now was how she could use her new strength to do good.

Whatever she had become, she took some comfort in knowing that she still had her mind and her soul. They hadn't been corrupted yet, which meant that she still had time to stop the last two knights before her transformation was complete and she was lost forever.

Kara spotted the bookstore. She dropped to the ground. Soft yellow light spilled from the edges of the boarded-up windows. She glanced down the street. Nothing. Most of the street's shops were still in ruin from the imp attack. A buzz came from a single street lamp. The old bookstore was surrounded by a bubble of quiet that told her the place was empty. Was she too late? Had Metatron gotten here first?"

But just when Kara was about to scream her frustration, the front door burst open.

"What took you so long?" Mr. Patterson's thin white hair was disheveled. His eyes were wide, and he panted like he had run a marathon.

"I've been waiting for *hours* since I heard about your encounter with Metatron. Quickly, get inside."

He looked past Kara's shoulders. "You never know what lurks in the shadows."

Without a word, Kara folded her wings behind her, stepped through the threshold and watched Mr. Patterson lock the door behind her.

"I thought you were gone," she said.

She was a little shocked to find him here and still in one piece.

"I thought I was too late." Without thinking, she pulled the old man into a hug.

Mr. Patterson giggled as if Kara had tickled him by accident. He pulled away from her with a huge smile.

"Well, they did come," said Mr. Patterson. "Those wretched angels with high heels and all that stuffy makeup. Why do they have to dress like that anyway? Well, I knew I'd be in a lot of trouble if they found me. I gather they know I'm responsible for sending you all after the knights."

"They do," said Kara. "I'm sorry, Mr. Patterson. I held on for as long as I could…but he literally had us cornered, and he knew it. He knew where we were. I think he'd figured it out when he confronted me in Horizon. It's my fault. I'm not as good a liar as I thought. Now, we've lost David and the others."

Mr. Patterson smiled tenderly. "Don't ever blame yourself for this my dear. None of this is your fault. Remember that. I'm just sorry it happened at all."

He sighed. "I wish we'd had more time, more guardians to help us. But I just couldn't take any chances with unfamiliar guardians. I'm not sure how much good it would have done anyway. He still discovered our plan."

Kara pressed her lips together. "What's the deal with Metatron anyway? He seems to have a vendetta against you."

Mr. Patterson blinked. "Well, my relationship with Metatron goes back a long time. We've never seen eye to eye. We're basically like cats and dogs. He gets under my skin. We just can't seem to agree on anything."

"Because you don't buy into his schemes."

"Precisely," said Mr. Patterson. "But understand, Metatron's not *bad*—not in the way a demon or an archfiend is bad. He's not a fallen archangel or a disloyal one. On the contrary, he's a little too loyal, too obsessed, and it makes him very dangerous as both an ally and as an enemy."

"Wonderful." Kara hated the guy. The next time she saw him she decided that she would feed him his cigar.

"So how did you escape from his clutches?" she asked. "It took me almost two hours to get here—"

"I know," said Mr. Patterson dramatically. "It was a very long time to be stuck in my little cupboard."

He saw that Kara looked confused. "I hid."

"You hid. Where?"

The old man crossed the room and made his way around his makeshift counter. She watched as he made a fist and punched the wall behind the counter. A small panel popped open and revealed a small room the size of a broom closet. It was large enough to fit two grown men, so there was plenty of space to fit an oracle. A shimmer caught her eye, and when she leaned in closer she saw a row of gleaming crystal balls tucked away neatly in a sky-blue blanket in a box on the floor. They looked like newborn babies cuddling together.

Kara suppressed a laugh. Who was she to judge anyway?

"My secret cupboard." Mr. Patterson beamed.

Kara smiled back at him. "A panic room. Brilliant."

A smug smile materialized on his face.

"Well, it wouldn't work if demon hounds were after me. They'd smell me a mile away. But it works for the average, lousy angel spy."

Kara inspected the small closet more closely. "This is great, but someone must have told you he was coming."

Mr. Patterson pulled the cupboard door shut. "Ariel did."

Kara's mouth dropped open.

"Ariel?" she repeated. She realized that there was much more to the archangel than she had given her credit for. She was grateful that Ariel had defied Metatron.

"But...I thought *Raphael* was one of your secret allies?"

"She is," said the oracle. "But Ariel had always been conflicted when it came to Metatron. She fears Metatron, and with good reason. But still, she believed your story about the demons. She told me so. But she couldn't defy Metatron openly, so this is her way of helping us."

Kara's spirits lifted. "I'm glad she did."

The old man watched her warily.

"Tell me," he ruffled the front of his shirt with his hands. "Are the four seals still intact? Ariel wasn't able to give me any information on that account."

Kara shook her head. "No. There are only two left."

There was no point in lying to the man. She dug a hand into her pant pocket and retrieved the small golden ring. She held it between two fingers and searched it to see if it had any power. And when she didn't find anything, she slipped it over her right ring finger. It felt right. No point in keeping her hands hidden now.

"Jenny and I still have our rings."

Mr. Patterson watched her silently.

"We tried. We really did. But the knights were wickedly strong. They have powers unlike anything I've ever faced before."

"What about your connection to them?" Mr. Patterson's eyes widened. "Any news on that score? Have you discovered anything new that could help us?"

Kara ruffled her wings in irritation. "Not really. But I know we *can* kill them."

She gave the old man a wicked smile. "I know it because some of the higher demons confirmed it."

She frowned at the memory of the way they had sneered and laughed at her. God she hated demons.

153

Mr. Patterson was very still as he asked, "What do you mean, they *confirmed* it?"

"Because they were there."

"What? I knew it! I knew it!"

He spat. His expression hardened, and he looked like a bulldog ready to fight.

"Those wretched, foul, double-crossing creatures."

He paced around the room, kicking and punching at invisible foes, all the while mumbling to himself. "Wait till I get my crystals. They'll wish they'd never been created! We'll see who's calling the shots! I've never..."

Kara watched silently as the old man's tantrum faded away. She stared at the black, spidery veins on her hands, but she couldn't look at them for more than a few seconds. They disgusted her. She disgusted her. But as she looked at herself, she realized that the demons hadn't been at all surprised at the black markings on her face and body. It was almost as though they had *expected* her to look that way...

But how was that possible? No one had known about her transformation, except for some of the archangels. She needed to find out more about the demons.

Finally, Mr. Patterson sighed loudly and flattened the top of his thin hair with his hands as he gathered his wits again. Kara was surprised to see how much anger still lingered in his eyes.

"Tell me exactly what they did," he asked.

"Just when I was about to destroy the knight, three higher demons came out of nowhere and tackled me. And when I pushed them off me, the knight was gone. It's obvious. They didn't want me near it. They didn't want me to kill it because they *knew* I could. They protected it *from* me and made sure it got away."

Kara shivered at the thought of the knight's foul body. She had been so close, so close to her own freedom.

"The demons aren't going to honor this treaty, you know," she said after a moment. "They're planning something...I can *feel* it."

Mr. Patterson narrowed his eyes. "I never believed for one minute they would. They're demons, after all. It's in their nature to be dishonest. They can't be trusted, and the legion was foolish in thinking that they could. I cannot blame them for trying, but I wish they would have listened to me."

Kara shrugged. "I don't get it. Why did the legion trust them in the first place? It's like the entire legion's gone mad, or they were hypnotized or something."

"Because desperate times call for desperate measures."

"You can say that again," said Kara indignantly.

The weight of their failed mission weighed heavily on her shoulders. Without the others she was on her own, and that terrified her. She feared that she would fall into the darkness more easily, since no one would be there to help pull her back to the light. And her light was running out.

"So what do we do about the legion?" asked Kara. "Will Ariel help us? Maybe with her and Raphael on our side, the legion will listen to us. They have to."

Mr. Patterson looked exhausted and frail. "And if by chance you had an audience with them, do you think they would ever believe you?"

Kara hung her head. "No, not me, of course not me. I was thinking *you* might tell them. You know, you're an oracle after all—"

"Ha!" Mr. Patterson choked on a laugh. "You give me too much credit, my dear girl. As the souls would have it, *I* cannot show my face in Horizon—not for quite some time I'm afraid."

His eyes twinkled with a hint of mischief. "I've already had a lengthy discussion with Metatron and the High Council about the treaty with the demons. They chose to ignore me and *all* the oracles, including the oracle mothers."

"What did the oracle mothers say?"

Mr. Patterson patted a round lump inside his front jacket pocket that Kara suspected to be a small crystal ball.

"They have seen many versions of the future. Many of them projected time lines that could occur and many of them end in our doom."

"But that can't be." Kara whirled on the little man. "You said we had a chance. You said if we destroyed the knights before they broke the seals, then we'd have a chance. You said!"

"Yes, yes, yes," said the little man, and he sighed loudly.

When he looked at Kara again, he gave her a little smile.

"The white oracle saw *another* version of the future. It was just one trifling strand of the future that differed from the others—the tiniest glimpse. But it was the *only* one that showed a better future. The only one that showed *life*."

Kara felt like she was going to explode in anticipation. "Which was the one you based your *theory* with the seals on, right? Well tell me already, I'm dying here."

He raised his chin and changed his voice to a high-pitched tone that Kara figured was his attempt at sounding female, but it only made him sound like he had a bad case of strep throat. He coughed and then said, "The only way to stop the archfiends is with the demise of the knight."

Kara frowned.

"Wait a minute. Something's not right. You said..."

She faltered. A ray of hope shone through her. She feared that if she spoke her thoughts out loud, then the spark of hope would diminish, because it was too good to be true...

"Hmmm?"

Kara spoke very carefully, as though she were addressing a young child.

"You said *knight*. Singular. Not *knights*."

"No, *she* said that."

Kara rolled her eyes and waved her hand at the old man frantically.

"I know. I know. I mean the white oracle said *knight*. Not *knights*—plural, right?" Her eyes widened impatiently as she encouraged him to answer.

Mr. Patterson pressed his lips into a hard line, his brows furrowed.

"That's right. She said knight. *The knight.* So? Why are you smiling like you won the lottery? What am I missing here?"

With her nerves tingling in excitement, Kara grabbed Mr. Patterson's head and kissed it. A tiny smile crept on his face, but he couldn't meet her eyes.

"Because, if I'm right," she said, trying to control the tremor in her voice, "and I have a feeling that I am, it means we only need to kill *one* knight for the future to change. Don't you get it! Just one! One miserable knight! I feel like someone's handed me an early Christmas present!"

Mr. Patterson looked distracted for a moment. "I love Christmas. This year, I was thinking about dressing up as Santa. Maybe you can be my helper!"

"Okay there, Santa. First we destroy a knight, and then maybe if all goes well you'll have your Christmas."

Kara wished silently that they all might share a Christmas. She bounced on her feet, feeling fifty pounds lighter. She forgot about her wings, the markings, and the darkness that flowed inside her like blood. She couldn't remember feeling this excited, this happy, and she wanted the feeling to last forever.

"This is it. This is our chance. We find one of the other two, Death or War—and we destroy it." She punched into her palm.

"Let's go with War," said Mr. Patterson.

He waddled over and disappeared behind his counter.

"Death is the strongest of the four knights."

His voice sounded muffled, as he rummaged through boxes.

"War is the lesser evil of the two. I wouldn't want to face Death, if I didn't have to. We will go after the one whom we stand a real chance to destroy. Together, we will end War."

"Together?" said Kara. "As in me and you?"

Mr. Patterson looked up from behind his counter. "Yes. Together."

He wrinkled his face.

"Why are you looking at me like that? I can fight. I'm a member of the legion, aren't I? I might not be a guardian per say, but I'm still a participant with skills. And I have many talents that you've never seen. You need me, so I'm coming with you."

"I'm sure you have many talents." Kara's voice was calm. "But the answer is *no*."

She couldn't risk harming the old oracle. If anything were to happen to him, she would never forgive herself.

Mr. Patterson raised a puffy white eyebrow. "It's not *your* decision to make."

He moved back from the counter, and Kara could see that his jacket and pant pockets were bulging with hidden items that Kara suspected were crystal balls. An assortment of daggers, chains, and one metal sword, hung from his leather belt. And in his right hand, he held a wooden staff with a gleaming crystal on top. The staff was taller than him, and he looked like a modern-day wizard.

Kara frowned. "It doesn't make a difference how many weapons you have, you're not coming."

"But I am." Mr. Patterson moved to her side.

"Whether you want to admit it or not, you need my help, Kara."

He eyed the veins on her face and her hands.

"I'm the only one who can help you if things get worse. You're changing, faster than I would have liked. I can feel a coldness in you, like a cold fire."

Kara lowered her eyes.

"And I can also feel that you are fighting it. I can feel it right now. And that alone gives me reason to hope. There is darkness there inside you, Kara, but there is also light."

His eyes sparkled.

"But not for long," mumbled Kara.

She stared at the floor. She could feel a tiny flame inside her, burning low. She had been fighting a constant inner battle to keep the light from burning out. But she didn't know for how much longer she could keep it up. At first the darkness had tried to sneak up and take control every hour or so. Now it was almost every fifteen minutes.

"I don't know how much time you have before your transformation is complete. And I'd rather not think about it now. But, if and when you turn, I'm the only one who can bring you back. I can help you control the urges and pull you back to us. You know it. I'm coming with you, whether you like it or not!"

Even though Kara knew the oracle was probably right, she still felt a pang in her chest at the thought of harm coming to him. But what other options did she have. None. She was separated from the rest of the group, a fugitive from the legion, and although she hated to admit it—she *needed* the old man. She didn't want to be alone.

"Fine," she said finally, trying to hide the gratitude she felt. "But stay behind me at all times, and don't do anything foolish."

"Nonsense, when have I ever done anything *foolish*," he said with a gleam in his eyes.

But then he became serious again.

"While I was waiting for you in my cupboard, I used my *talents*, and I was able to pin point the knight's location."

"Where?"

"Well, if I'm right, he's in Mexico right now. But I don't know how long he's going to stay there."

Mexico. Kara didn't know how long it would take her to fly there. She couldn't return to Horizon and use the Vega tanks. It would take at least five hours, if not more, and that's if all went well. She wasn't even sure that she could make the trip without succumbing to the evil that threatened her at every second.

Mr. Patterson shook his head, and Kara could see that he was almost overcome with pain and sorrow.

"He started in Russia and then spread his evil to the lower parts of Europe and Africa. The wars he's created will kill millions of poor souls. Their minds have been corrupted by an evil they can't control. They don't know what they are doing. They're like puppets doing the devil's work. In a day or two, there may be nothing left. No souls to save and no world."

He fell silent for a moment.

"Right now, we have more important matters. The legion will go to war in a few hours."

He lifted a hand as Kara started to protest.

"And if we want to save them, we go now."

The oracle nodded and then said, "We must take hold of the future, before the future takes hold of us."

Kara made her way toward the front door and then whirled around. "Wait. I can fly there, but how are *you* going to get to Mexico?"

The oracle grinned. "I thought you could carry me?"

Kara's mouth fell open. "What?"

"Well, I'm in a pickle, aren't I?" said the little man. "I cannot go back to Horizon, and all air transportation has been grounded. So the only way I can get there is if you take me with you. I'm not very big, so I don't think I'll be a burden to you at all."

At first Kara thought the old man had gone mad. But as she stood staring at his determined old face, she realized that it wasn't such a foolish request. He probably didn't weigh more than ninety pounds. He wouldn't slow her down.

Mr. Patterson saw that she was considering it.

"I could climb on your back. That way I wouldn't obstruct your flying in any way. I'm not very heavy, I promise."

Kara decided that she would do whatever it took.

"Fine." Kara smiled. "Just pray to the souls no one we know *sees* us."

Kara pulled open the front door.

Salthazar and a mob of higher demons stood in the middle of the street.

CHAPTER 14

THE DEMISE

"I thought I'd find you here," said the demon lord.

His too-white teeth sparkled in the dim light as he stared at her with a mixture of awe and disbelief. "You look fantastic!"

Kara stiffened. "Are you coming on to me?"

She spat. "Sorry, but you're not my type."

Salthazar laughed softly, his handsome face too perfect to be human. "But I will be your *type* sooner than you think, and then you'll change your mind."

"You're delusional." Kara didn't know whether to laugh or punch him in the face. *Who did this guy think he was, anyway?* Even if he was disturbingly handsome, in a demon lord kind of way, she belonged with David until the end.

There must have been about a hundred demons standing behind him, and she could sense their pent-up ire and aggression.

Strangely enough, she felt rather proud that Salthazar felt they needed so many reinforcements. It meant they were afraid of her. She smiled wickedly.

"What do you want?" Kara saw Mr. Patterson reach for his dagger.

Salthazar smiled. "Isn't it obvious?"

He laughed softly again. "It's _you_ I've come for."

"If this is a marriage proposal, it really sucks."

The demon lord didn't lose his smile.

"You see, Kara, as much as I _like_ you and admire what you've become, I have to follow orders, just like you. And I just cannot have you flying all over this mortal world and ruining our plans."

At last Kara was going to find out what game the demons were playing. "Which is what, exactly?"

"You're in the way. I can't let you get close to any of the knights, not again. You got too close the last time, and I can't allow you to hurt them, let alone destroy them."

Kara growled. "So I was right. You want to _stop_ us from _killing_ those monstrosities. You know that if we kill one of them, your masters' plan will fail, and they will go back to their prison."

Salthazar's face slacked, but he didn't answer.

Kara glanced over to the oracle. He had been right all along. The white oracle had seen it.

"Don't answer," said Kara as she turned her attention back to the demon lord.

"But I know I'm right. Just the fact that you showed up here with your army of grunts to stop me, like you said, is all the proof I need."

She smiled wickedly. "You know I could destroy the knights, and that's why you're here. You're afraid I might win."

"Never start a war that you cannot win," said the demon lord with a savagery that twisted his handsome face.

Kara's cold rage started to rise again, and she pressed it down. "You lied to the legion. There never was a treaty, was there? You played us."

Salthazar's black eyes gleamed. "I did. And it was the easiest game of chess I've ever played. How could I say no? I couldn't. I'll rule the Netherworld with an unlimited supply of human souls? It was too good a deal to pass."

"You're scum."

"The legion chose to ignore their basic principles and sided with us. They fear the archfiends, and they succumbed to that fear. It's their loss now. And when they realize their folly, when they realize that I deceived them—it'll be too late."

"Not if I can help it." Kara wanted to claw his pretty face. Not now. Not yet.

"Well, it won't matter in the end," continued Salthazar calmly. "Either way it won't change the fact that I just can't let you out of my sight. You will never get near the knights again."

"Try and stop me."

The demon lord sneered. "I will."

Salthazar snapped his fingers.

The demons charged.

"Get behind me," she growled at Mr. Patterson as she shielded his body with hers.

She was ready for more bloodshed. She was looking forward to it. Let them come. She didn't have to tap into her cool, dark power. It was already coursing through her body.

They came at her, blades swinging. She met their weapons with her own blade, ducking and blocking faster and with more skill than she ever thought possible, another gift from the darkness, no doubt. But she didn't have time to admire her abilities. She needed to get herself and Mr. Patterson out before things got more ugly and dangerous for the both of them.

She met their daggers and swords with strength and agility, spinning and moving through the mass of demons like a skilled dancer. She used her wings, now that she knew she could, and sliced though their limbs and watched them fall like broken branches. Steel flashed. Demons hissed and screamed. The air was filled with the sounds of ringing metal and the shouts of dying demons. She soared through them easily, relishing the savagery of her darkness.

With one rapid movement, she hurled her sword at a demon who had thrown his blade at her and missed. Black blood seeped from his mouth and from the deep gouge in his neck before he fell over like a dead tree. She pulled out her blade and kicked away the body.

Another one came at her and knocked her aside with a powerful blow to the head. Kara stumbled backward, but she was up again in an instant. She flipped her dagger in her hand, caught it by the tip of the blade, and flung it straight into the creature's eye. Before the demon even had time to crumple to the ground, she pulled out her blade and jumped over its disintegrating body.

She wondered if Salthazar was still smiling.

Ten more demons came at her at once. Too fast. Before she could react, she was slammed into a wall and pain burst from her shoulder as her wings were crushed with a sickening crack.

"Don't kill her!"

She heard Salthazar's voice over the rumble of the battle.

"I need her *alive* and unscathed."

Kara couldn't fathom why the demon lord didn't just kill her. The thought that he was infatuated with her was repulsive. Whatever his reason, it gave her an advantage. If they didn't want her destroyed, then this would be easier than she thought.

Groaning, she glimpsed down. Three death blades punctured her abdomen with wounds that would have committed any normal angel to a miserable and agonizing true death. She was surprised that she felt the pain, but *not* the burning poison she had felt so many times before. She should be dying right about now. So why was it not happening? Were their blades defective? Even the pain wasn't what it should be. It should have hurt a heck of a lot more. It was almost like the death blades' poison didn't affect her. Not anymore.

Whatever the darkness had done to protect her, she would thank it later.

She kicked out hard, and two higher demons went sprawling. She saw an opening and thrust the tip of her left wing into another demon's head, perforating it like a pumpkin. Another one came, and she spun and side kicked it in the chest. Two death blades came flying at her, swinging like karate nunchucks. She ducked, but the blades chopped off a piece of her wing.

Kara rolled on the ground, howling in pain. The drips of black blood on the ground were her blood this time.

She cried a scream that came from deep within her soul. She cursed the black blood, and the monster she was becoming. With black blood dripping from her wounds, she snarled and attacked anything that came near her. Slicing. Thrashing. Biting. She was snarling like a wild animal. In her rage, she saw nothing but darkness and blood. She wanted only to kill.

She had become a killing machine.

She caught a glimpse at Salthazar.

He was smiling. It was like he enjoyed watching her kill his own demons.

In her rage she had forgotten the oracle.

Her insides froze. She saw that Mr. Patterson was pushed up against the front door of his bookstore. He was trapped by seven demons. The fear in his eyes sent a chill down her back. She had to get to him. She had to get him out.

With her face and hands caked with the blood of her enemies, she thrashed like a wild creature cutting a path through the horde of demons. Their faces blurred as she ploughed her way toward Mr. Patterson.

169

Blinding pain erupted from the side of her head, and wetness fell into her eyes, but she didn't stop. She couldn't stop. She had to reach him—

She heard the oracle scream.

Frantic, she screamed louder and drove her dagger into the eye of the last higher demon in her way. She was almost there.

And then what she saw was like in slow motion. She saw four of the demons pull their death blades out of the oracle's chest. His blue eyes met hers in a silent plea, almost as though he was sorry. And then he staggered. His knees buckled beneath him, and he fell over.

"NO!"

Kara bounded to him and spun like a wild tornado. The severed bodies of the demons fell around her as she fell to her knees sobbing.

"No, no, no," she cried.

She pressed her hands over his wounds, and silver liquid seeped through her fingers. There was so much of it. She knelt in the pool of his essence.

He opened his mouth and silver essence poured from the corners. "I'm—sorry."

His eyes glazed over and became lifeless.

The higher demons circled her, but she just knelt there. Her hands trembled, and she sobbed uncontrollably.

"Mr. Patterson? Mr. Patterson?"

His body moved, a bit of hope, but then she realized it was her shaking that had caused the movement. The vibrant, fierce, loving soul, the one person who had looked after her like a real father, who had taken care of her, whose shop had been like a beacon of hope, was gone.

The oracle was dead.

Kara stared at his body. She was numb. She was lost.

Why hadn't his soul appeared?

And then something hard hit the back of her head and everything went dark.

CHAPTER 15

CAGED

When Kara came to, she was blindfolded. Her head still throbbed from the blow she had received, and she didn't know how long she had been unconscious or where she was. But she didn't care. There was only darkness. Darkness inside her. Darkness around her. And she welcomed it. She *deserved* it.

She had gotten Mr. Patterson killed. If she had surrendered herself to Metatron, the oracle would still be alive. If only she had followed the rules for once. But now he was dead, and it was her fault. She always thought that she knew better than anyone else. How could she, when in Horizon years she was practically a newborn.

She should have taken the punishment and gone to Tartarus, but she'd fled like a coward. She *was* a coward. People died in her wake. She was a coward and a monster.

Didn't Mr. Patterson see this coming in his crystal balls? Why hadn't he told her? She wished he'd stayed hidden in his cupboard.

Kara stifled a cry. It wasn't his fault. It was hers. It was not his familiar smiling face she saw beneath her blindfold but the pained and frightened face of a friend as his life slipped away.

What happened to oracles when they suffered their true death? Was it like the angels? Did their souls reincarnate into another oracle?

The more she thought about it, the more she realized she didn't know much at all about the other beings in Horizon. She had never really cared. She was selfish. He had died in vain, and it was all her fault. Let her own true death come, she wanted it.

She lay on a hard stone floor. Water trickled in the distance. The air was damp, and it smelled of sulfur, rot and toxic gas. At first, it reminded her of Tartarus, but it *felt* different. It was hot, too hot to be Tartarus. And what limited air there was, was choking hot, suffocating. Wherever she was, a mortal couldn't survive here.

And it wasn't the Netherworld either. She still felt the pulls of the mortal world. She was still on Earth, but she just didn't know where.

The ground pulsed against her cheek like it had a beating heart, like it was alive. Even lying down, she felt a hot wind blow in and out with a tempo like it was breathing. It was creepy but it faded away like remnants of a dream as she fell in and out of consciousness.

After lying down for what felt like hours, she tried to move her arms. They were bound and so were her feet. Rope. If she wanted to, she could find a way to rip her bonds apart. But she didn't want to. She deserved this. All of it.

She crawled on her hands and knees until her head hit something solid. A wall. She managed to turn herself around and sat with her back to the wall. Her head still throbbed, and she could feel the nasty bump where she had been hit.

She had nothing left to give. With the death of the oracle, she had inadvertently become the monster she feared. It had been inevitable, just as Salthazar had said. She was meant to become this monster.

She would die in the bleakness of this place, in her own hell, alone and forgotten.

"I killed Mr. Patterson," she whispered in the dark, needing someone or something to hear her confession. "I killed him."

Had the white oracle seen this part of the future?

She didn't understand why Salthazar hadn't ended her right then and there back at the bookstore. It would have been really easy for him. But he didn't. And now she was here, somewhere, as their captive. But why?

The two remaining seals were probably broken by now. And what was the point in even thinking about it? It was all over. The angels would be annihilated and billions of mortals would be dead. Horizon would be destroyed, and there would be nothing left. She tried hard not to think about it.

A door scraped open somewhere nearby. She heard hushed voices, and then heavy tread of feet approached her. She kept her head down.

"Finally. You're conscious." It was Salthazar's voice. He sounded as though he'd been waiting a very long time for her to wake up.

"You've been out for nearly an entire *day*."

Kara frowned. *Why was that important to her?* She felt that it should be, but she couldn't remember why. She let the question dissolve.

"They shouldn't have hit you so hard." The demon lord sounded irritated this time. *Was that a hint of concern she detected?*

"I was getting a little worried. But what's done is done, and now you're up. I'm very happy to see you well again, *Kara*."

Kara snarled at the way he said her name, like he longed for her. It disgusted her. Did he think they were somehow going to be an item? If he did, then he was delusional. She didn't want anything except for an end to her miserable life.

"Why don't you just kill me and get on with it," she growled.

Her voice was raw, like she'd swallowed a glass full of razor blades. "I'm no use to you...or to anyone."

Kara could hear boots on the stone floor nearby.

"Kill you?" Salthazar was right next to her. "Whatever gave you that idea? We *don't* want to kill you...*I* don't want to kill you."

He paused, and Kara thought she heard him lick his lips.

"I can see now that all the rumors about you are true. You may just be glorious now...but you will be magnificent. You were always destined to be great. Your father knew it, and I know it. Even the dark gods know it. And you were always destined to be on *our* side—*not* the angels. You know that I speak the truth."

175

Kara grunted. She wanted him to shut up.

"What I mean to say is that angels and demons are practically the same. We are all spawn from the same supernatural creators. We are all built the same way, and we all have the same abilities and desires. Mortals worship the angels, and the angels want that. We want it too, is that so wrong? Of course not. Why shouldn't we be worshiped alongside the angels? We are just a different kind of angel, if you will, a better kind. A stronger kind. And you're one of us."

"Join us," said the demon lord.

He was so close now that he must be kneeling beside her.

"Join me, Kara. I'll take care of you. You'll be worshiped by my side for all eternity. You and I are equals. We can rule them all, my darling."

Kara felt a cold finger brush her cheek.

"You are even more beautiful now than any creature in all the worlds," he crooned.

His hand was in her hair now and slowly making its slippery way to her wings.

"Embrace the darkness. Don't fight it, my darling."

Kara didn't even flinch as his fingers continued to inspect her body. She was numb. Her soul was numb, and she didn't care. She could only see the oracle's terrified face.

It would have been better if her father, Asmodeus, had killed her that night in the cemetery. Better to have suffered her true death there. Her body didn't feel like it was hers anymore. Her light was nearly extinguished, and she sensed that the darkness of her transformation was almost complete. She didn't fight it anymore. She let it come.

She guessed that she wasn't reacting the way that the demon lord had anticipated because after a moment, he removed his hand, and she heard him pacing over the damp stones.

Were they in a cave?

The pacing stopped.

"If I let you out, promise you'll behave?" purred the demon lord.

Kara slowly lifted her chin, straining to hear anything familiar that might help her pinpoint her location.

"I hate having you locked up in here. Your place is by my side. We will rule the Netherworld together."

Salthazar paced around again.

"I want you to *see*. I want you to see and hear those lying angels as they squirm and beg for their lives. Together we will tear their souls apart."

Kara's head felt heavy. She felt drained and tired.

What was this idiot mumbling about? Why couldn't he just shut up and kill her already? "Get her up," commanded Salthazar. "And remove the blindfold. I want her to *see* everything."

Kara was about to argue that he should leave it on, but the bonds that tied her feet were cut, and the blindfold was pulled off her face.

She blinked the black spots from her eyes as Salthazar lifted her to her feet and steadied her. She was surprised to find that she could actually stand. Her wings were still bound with rope.

As her vision cleared, she took in her surroundings. Black, glimmering walls surrounded her in a space the size of her small bedroom. But this was no bedroom—it was a prison cell in a cave or dungeon. She was a bird with clipped wings, and she would never to fly again. She accepted her fate. It would all be over soon enough.

Salthazar was only accompanied by two higher demons. They didn't seem to regard her as much of a threat to them anymore.

She looked down. Her hands were caked with black demon blood, but there was also silver blood mixed in with it. It was smeared over her hands and fingers. She still had the oracle's blood on her. She resisted the urge to cry.

The two higher demons held her firmly by her arms.

Why was it so hot?

"Forgive me, my darling, but I cannot remove the bonds around your hands," said Salthazar. "Not yet. But soon, I promise. I suspect that you still have remnants of angel deep inside you. But once you are fully converted, you will join me in battle. You will be magnificent to watch. You will be perfection."

Kara wrinkled her nose at the reek of his strong, musky cologne. It was almost like he was trying to mask the stink of rot and death that demons naturally exude. It wasn't working. It only accentuated the smell even more.

What was his problem? Was he trying to seduce her with his perfume?

He stood so close to her that she wondered if she smelled like a demon now, too. His black eyes rolled over her ever so slowly.

Handsome as he was, his eyes were still unsettling and unnatural. She looked away.

"The dark gods have asked for you," said Salthazar.

He straightened his shoulders proudly. "So, naturally, I have to keep you bound for now. I can't risk you doing anything foolish and embarrassing me. But they'll come off, once you've proven yourself worthy to be a child of darkness."

She wished he would stop talking.

"I know you can't see it now. You can't imagine what it would be like to have limitless power."

Salthazar's voice rose with excitement as his lust for power revealed itself. He reminded Kara of her father.

"But you will, and you will embrace it."

"Why do they want to see me?" Her voice was a whisper.

She stared at the blood on her hands, and her knees buckled at the shame. But the higher demons pulled her back up and shook her awake as though she had fallen asleep.

Salthazar made for the door of her cell.

"Don't parents yearn to see their young? The dark gods have waited long enough. We've wasted enough time with your beauty sleep. When you are fully recovered, and your mind is focused, you will take your rightful place and fight alongside your *true* family."

Kara squirmed at the word. She had already lost one member of her family. She would carry the weight of his death forever.

The demon lord's black eyes sparkled in delight.

"Enjoy your last moments as an angel, my darling, because they won't last. Soon you will feast your eyes on the new world where we will reign as king and queen. It has already begun."

Kara had no idea what he was mumbling about, but she felt obligated to ask.

"What has?"

Salthazar halted outside the cell. He turned with a sly smile on his face and said excitedly, "The war of the worlds."

CHAPTER 16
THE ARCHFIENDS

The higher demons dragged Kara through dim corridors carved into the same black rock as her cell. Smoky torches on the walls of these great gloomy caves were the only source of light, and Kara peered through the smoke to try and figure out where she was. They climbed higher and higher through a confusing network of tunnels, and the smell of death clung to her skin like a mist. She could almost taste it in her mouth.

Kara kept her face blank as she asked, "What is this place?"

"Mexico," said Salthazar brightly.

He walked a few paces in front of her. "At the root of the Popocatépetl volcano. But don't worry, it's not *active*...well, not right now anyway."

So she had made it to Mexico after all. Now she understood why it was so hot. Demons or not, Kara was pretty sure that they weren't immune to scorching lava. If this was some sort of demon safe house, it wasn't exactly safe. But she had to give Salthazar points for originality. Then again, he had mentioned earlier that he was taking her to see the archfiends, so maybe this wasn't exactly a hideout. Maybe it was the archfiends' lair.

"How did I get here?" she grunted after a moment. If this was the archfiends lair, she didn't want to see it or be in it. They should have left her in her cell.

Salthazar watched her for a moment. She hated the desire in his black eyes. It made her feel dirty. He seemed convinced that they would be together in the future. She still wanted to claw his eyes out.

Kara saw a smile on his lips.

"You have more of *us* in you than you think. Things are changing for you, Kara. Your fiend essence, or whatever you want to call it, allowed you to move through rifts with us. Your body no longer needs to replenish itself outside the veils. It's stronger. You're stronger."

He paused. "You'll see. It gets better."

The higher demons on each side of her laughed. She glanced at them all, one after the other, and was disturbed by the dark shadows that danced on their identical faces as they smiled at her. They were enjoying this a little too much.

Kara didn't want to know what *got better*. Just the thought of becoming more demon, or whatever she was, than angel made her feel like her soul was being ripped away from her body—she was losing her true self. The suffocating darkness was devouring her soul. It was that fear she had struggled with since the very beginning of her training with the legion. She had been marked since the very beginning.

But she deserved what she got. All of it.

Thousands of red and yellow eyes watched her from the shadows as she trudged along behind Salthazar. Normally, she would have been apprehensive, but now she didn't care. Ghoulish creatures with corrupted bodies covered with sores stalked along the edges of the tunnel beside her, hissing and cursing her in an ancient language.

A wall shimmered to her left, and a great horned demon with purple, scaly skin and two pairs of arms walked through the rift on hooves the size of car wheels. His four white-milky eyes settled on Kara. His maw opened as he growled at her, but one look from Salthazar and the creature retreated into the shadows.

All along the tunnels more and more rifts rippled open and spit out creatures with dripping maws and twisted, pulsing bodies. It was like an underworld train station.

Some of the creatures were the size of elephants. Others were smaller. Gray dwarf creatures appeared from puffs of black smoke and hurried down the tunnels. Imps. She'd never forget what they had done to Peter. She shook her head so she wouldn't dwell on her friends and forced herself to focus on the lower demons. They all moved with quiet purpose as they marched together in lines and disappeared down various tunnels.

As they climbed, she couldn't tell if these tunnels were natural or manmade, but she could feel the rumbling under her feet increase. Eventually the reverberation was coming from everywhere at once. And over the sound of the tremors and the tread of their feet, Kara could hear muffled sounds from above. It sounded like the clatter of steel against steel.

The reek of sulfur had burned her nose when she was in her cell, but as they climbed higher, the sulfur became more bearable. But the echoes of clashing steel grew stronger.

After what felt like hours of climbing, the gloom thinned, and Kara could see a wall of soft yellow light at the end of the tunnel. Kara followed Salthazar into the light.

At first, the bright light was so intense she had to cover her eyes with her hands. But as she blinked, her eyes gradually adjusted.

She stood near a platform on the lip of a ravine that led down to a vast desert hundreds of feet below. Thousands of higher demons, shadow demons, clowns demons, hound demons, imps and other devilings and creatures she'd never seen before crowded the cliffs around her.

Near the edge of the platform on a raised stone dais, seven archfiends sat on seven black marble thrones. They looked out over the desert below from their ledge where the mountain opened up to a clouded gray sky.

The sounds of battle raged from somewhere down below the ledge, but the platform was still, and the archfiends sat and watched.

When Kara had imagined them, she had assumed they would be big, menacing humanoid monsters. She wasn't prepared at all for what she saw.

There were four males and three females, and they all wore crowns made of black diamond. They radiated dark power.

Even in the soft light, they were cloaked in shadow. Black veins pulsed under their gray-colored skin, and their long black tresses hung over their chests. The females wore metal armor around their chests, but the males' muscular torsos were bare. They wore golden loops in their ears. Long necklaces hung from their necks, and too many rings glimmered on their fingers. They were kingly and terrifying.

But the thing that disturbed Kara the most was that they all had wings just like hers. She couldn't miss them. Their giant leathery black wings were like the wings of dragons.

Their thrones faced out from the mountain's ledge, and the archfiends were fixated on something down below. But before she could see what they were looking at, the higher demons dragged her toward the center of the platform.

The male archfiend in the middle differed from all the rest. He was nearly a head taller than the other males, and he clutched a globe in his hands. Kara could see that the globe represented the mortal world.

Slowly, the archfiends turned their heads and watched her with great interest as she made her way across the platform. The higher demons' grips tightened around her arms as they steadied her, and she stood facing the archfiends.

"My lords and ladies," Salthazar groveled before the archfiends. "My gods and goddesses."

Kara clenched her jaw and rolled her eyes. He was pathetic. Didn't demons have any pride?

The archfiends watched Salthazar with faces as expressionless as stone masks.

Kara took the opportunity to look around. Half a dozen men and women stood to the left and right of the thrones. They looked like bodyguards, although Kara had the feeling that the archfiends didn't need them. The bodyguards had unsettling large yellow eyes with slit-like irises, like cats. Their black veins shone under their paper-white skin like tattoos, and they wore long black cloaks. Kara could see the strong bodies they hid beneath. Their features were perfect.

One of them in particular caused a shudder to pass through her. She recognized him at once.

He was tall and thin, and he smiled at her with a mouthful of black needle-like teeth.

It was the same man who had injected her with the syringe when she had run through the woods in search of David. It had been his needle that had started her mutation.

She cringed when she realized that all the archfiends were glaring at her.

"Kneel before your gods," growled the archfiend in the middle.

Kara immediately took him to be their commander. His voice thundered and cracked, and she felt it resonate inside her core. But she met his stare and wouldn't look away. It was stupid, she knew, but right now she didn't care.

Shouting erupted from below the ledge where the archfiend had been watching. They were screams, and they definitely weren't the screams of demons.

She turned to look, but Salthazar backhanded her.

"Lord Beelzebub told you to kneel," ordered Salthazar.

Her cheek seared in pain, but she wouldn't kneel. She stood her ground and challenged them to make her kneel.

Beelzebub looked furious, but Kara didn't alter her stone-cold expression.

Salthazar cursed, and then he kicked her feet from under her. Kara went down hard in a tangle of her limbs and wings.

"Bow to your new masters, darling," hissed Salthazar.

Then he added, very low, so that only she could her, "Because if you don't, we're both dead."

Kara didn't care about the demon lord or these giant scary archfiends. She stood up stubbornly, her chin high in defiance, and said, "I don't kneel to demons."

The archfiends shouted and pounded their fists on their thrones. They bared their black pointy teeth in feral snarls. The shadows around their thrones darkened until the entire mountain went dark, and the air burned hot and smelled of sulfur.

Beelzebub raised his hand.

"You insult us gravely," said the archfiend. "We are your gods. We created you! And you dare to insult us? Is this how you repay those who have given you more power than any other worldly creature?"

It all made sense now. These were the creatures behind her mutation. They were the ones who had destroyed her spirit. She would never thank them for what they had done to her. They had destroyed her.

Kara stood with her chin in the air.

The archfiend examined her face and her wings. A frown materialized on his pale brow.

"You should have been fully changed by now."

"Glad to disappoint you—"

One of the high demons punched her in the stomach.

She groaned and then straightened very slowly. She made a mental note to kill the demon once her bonds were free.

"Something is slowing the process down," said the dark god. "Perhaps we overlooked something. Perhaps it'll just take a little longer until you become—"

"A demon like them?"

Kara directed her bound hands at the creatures standing next to the thrones.

"I'd rather you'd kill me right now. You have your escorts and your bodyguards. You don't need me."

She could see that Salthazar looked frightened, but she couldn't tell whether it was fear for her, or fear for himself.

"If my lord will permit me," said the demon creature that she'd recognized from the woods.

Beelzebub gave a slight nod, and the creature turned to Kara.

"*We*," he raised his arms to indicate that he meant the other beings next to him, "are *not* demons, girl. We're much more complex and stronger than mere demons. We outrank them. We are superior to all lesser creatures. We are fiends."

Salthazar's expression darkened.

Kara shrugged. "Demons...fiends...I don't care. To me, you're all the same. Evil."

She glared at the fiend who had injected her.

"But you...you're the worst." She tried to free her wings, but they were held tight. "You did this to me."

"I'm called Betaazu—"

"There are a few names I'd like to call you."

Betaazu didn't flinch. His face was as blank as the stone floor. He made a move toward her, but he halted at the archfiends' glare.

"Wait," said Beelzebub, "she might still be useful in her angel body. Let's not spoil her just yet. I'm curious."

Lord Beelzebub was silent for a moment. He seemed to be thinking. He fiddled with the globe in his hand, and then he turned his eyes on Kara.

Something moved in her peripheral vision. Three giant knights had appeared quickly and silently behind her, and now they sat on their great steeds, expressionless beneath their metal helmets, just like their creators. *How could she have not seen them arrive?* They were enormous.

There was one she'd never see before, a red knight. Even his steed was red. Just like the other knights, he was clad in red armor that hid most of this monstrous and muscular body. He glared at Kara with loathing. The knights sat silently, watching and waiting. *But for what?*

Where was the fourth knight? Kara couldn't see the knight called Death.

She didn't care.

She heard the scraping crunch of footsteps on pebbles behind her. She turned around, and her smile faded.

A crowd of men, women, and children came stumbling through one of the tunnels. Their hands and feet were shackled. Their clothes were ripped and stiff with their own blood, and they were covered in cuts and bruises. Many of them wept, and they cowered as they dragged their chains into the chamber. They looked horrified when they saw the archfiends. Children cried. Their faces were streaked with dirt and dried tears.

Her nose burned at the reek of them. They smelled of fear and death. They were human slaves. It was a glimpse of what the world would be like if the archfiends were not stopped.

Kara's head pounded more savagely than before as unyielding rage boiled up inside her.

"What is the meaning of this?" Kara bit back her anger.

Betaazu appeared to relish her rage. He smiled and said, "Human initiation, an introduction to their new gods."

Kara looked at a little girl, no more than eight years old.

"Slaves," she hissed. "Human slaves. Isn't it enough that you've plagued them with disease, starvation, and war? Now you've taken those who've managed to survive and made them into slaves. It's sick."

"It's a new regime. A cleansing. The humans that survive will have to obey and worship their new gods. There's no other choice for them."

Kara watched as the human slaves were prodded into position by a group of imps. The imps yanked and pulled on the mortals' chains, laughing and taunting them with sticks and whips. The crimson stains on the imps' hands and knuckles left Kara with no doubt that they had tortured these poor souls. The slaves formed a straight line facing the archfiends. The imps bowed low and waited.

A male fiend with a shaved head moved forward. "Renounce your old ways and embrace the future. Kneel and worship your dark gods."

The slaves didn't move. Maybe they were too afraid to move, or too shocked. Kara had the feeling that some of them were about to faint. She didn't know what they had gone through. It must have been terrible. But still none of the slaves moved.

"Kneel before the gods," commanded the fiend. "Choose the dark gods and live...or chose death."

One of the mothers was the first to kneel. She clung to her children and pulled them down with her. And then all the other bent and broken slaves kneeled, too. All except one.

An elderly man covered in angry blue and purple bruises stood his ground. His white hair was caked in blood. He reminded her of Mr. Patterson, and she bit down on her lip.

"Kneel, Frank," whispered one of the men.

"Do it. It's not worth your life," he said in a low voice.

But Frank didn't move. "It is to me."

The other man shook his head sadly but didn't speak again. The other slaves kept their heads low and their eyes on the ground.

The male fiend was at Frank's side faster than Kara had time to blink.

"You worthless human! How dare you be impertinent before your gods, human? You insolent, miserable mortal scum. Kneel! Kneel before the dark gods!"

The old man held his head high and squared his shoulders.

"I will not. I never believed in this hocus-pocus before. I can't deny that I've seen things that I can never explain, and that I don't understand. But this…"

The man raised his chained wrists and gestured toward the fiends.

"…I can see now that there are both good and evil forces in the universe. You claim to be gods? I don't know if that is true, but my heart tells me that you are not gods, but devils. I don't know what you are, or why you are here. But if I did believe in a god, it would be a just god, a kind god. It would not be a god that kills and forces the weak to worship him."

"If you don't kneel now, old fool," whispered the fiend, "you will die. I promise you."

Frank's old eyes twinkled with tears. "I don't fear death because I believe our spirits live on."

"Infidel!" cried the fiend. "Useless bag of blood."

He punched the old man in the stomach so hard that he keeled over and blood spilled from his mouth.

"Stop! How dare you!" Kara surged forward but was pulled back sharply by Betaazu. She thrashed and kicked in his hold, but he didn't let go.

The fiend lifted the old man by the neck and dragged him to the edge of the ravine.

The man cried out and fought as hard as his old limbs and strength would allow. But he was no match for the supernatural strength of the fiend.

With a final struggle the fiend tossed the old man over the ledge. His scream rang in Kara's ears, her knees trembled, and then she heard him no more.

A low growl slipped through her teeth as a wild fury seized her.

"Let go of me," she snarled.

She yanked hard, but the demon held firm.

"Monsters! You monsters! I'll kill you. I'll kill you all!"

In a single, swift movement, she twirled behind the demon. His grip faltered, and she jumped back, ready to run at the murderous fiend, but Betaazu caught her again easily.

"Stop moving or I'll break it," he snarled. "Or I'll throw you over, too."

"Do it," she spat. "Throw me over, *demon*."

The muscles in his jaw tightened. "Don't push me."

But she did. She swept her leg into the back of his knees, and he fell. He didn't release her as they hit the ground, and she landed on top of him.

Betaazu seemed pleased. "I must say that I like this very much."

If her hands hadn't been bound, she would have punched him. But she made do and ploughed her elbow into his face.

The demon lord cursed as he flipped her on her back. She knocked her head on the hard stony surface and saw stars. He leapt to his feet and tried to pull her to her feet again, but she kicked him hard in the stomach. She made her way to tackle him, but he caught her by the shoulder and threw her to the ground again. Then he kicked her in the face, grabbed her wrists, and pinned her to the ground.

"Enough," he growled. "There's no point to this. I'll always win. You're outmatched, Kara. Just give it up."

Kara thrashed under his grasp and finally gave up. Only when she stopped did he pull her back to her feet.

Kara looked at the slaves. They were watching her, pleading for her help. But she was trapped and shackled, a slave just like them.

And there was nothing she could do about it.

Kara looked away from them and tried to hide her own fear.

Could they see that she was an angel? Is that why they pleaded with her silently? Did they know what she was? But how could they?

Perhaps the supernatural veil that had prevented humans from seeing angels had been lifted from their eyes by the archfiends. It wouldn't matter anyway. The monster inside her had devoured every last trace of her angel essence and left only a beast in its wake.

But what if she was wrong?

Perhaps the mortals had *seen* something good in her. After all they had sought her out. They had asked for her help. They knew something. They could see something in her. She had sworn to protect them. *Could they read it in her eyes?*

It had taken all her strength to fight off Betaazu.

Maybe she had already given up. Maybe she hadn't fought as hard as she might have because deep down she knew it was pointless.

Kara watched the imps lead the human slaves away down another tunnel. A child let out a whimper, and Kara's essence began to boil again.

She looked at her hand and gave a little gasp. A small flicker of gold winked at her from her finger.

Kara had forgotten her ring. Maybe it could give her the answers that she needed. Doing her best not to look too conspicuous, she glanced down at the ring again.

One of the seals must still have been unbroken.

A mischievous smile spread on her lips. There was still a chance to save them all.

And then something inside Kara awoke.

CHAPTER 17

A TUMBLE OF FIENDS

It was sudden. The tiny light inside her pulsed and grew. Her head began to clear. She didn't want to die anymore. She wanted to fight. There was still a fight left in her, whether it was angel or not, it didn't matter. What mattered was what she'd do with it. She held on to that feeling. A veil had been lifted, not just from her mind but from her eyes. She could *see* now. She could see everything. Maybe it was a result of becoming a monster, but she seemed to have developed some sort of sixth sense and x-ray vision. Everything had slowed down around her, and her perceptions had sharpened.

She noticed something strange about the archfiends. Something was *off*—they were off. Their bodies seemed to shimmer and fade, like ghosts or wraiths that were constantly struggling to stay solid. It was as though part of them belonged somewhere else...

Mr. Patterson had said that the archfiends' powers were lessened on Earth because of the lengthy duration of their imprisonment. Somehow they were still *linked* to their prison by the seals that had kept them confined. To gain full control over their powers, they would literally have to break out of their cage.

The more she observed, the more clearly she could see it. Their skin was semi-transparent. It was a subtle shift, but it reminded her of when she had begun to fade.

They hadn't fully broken out yet! They wouldn't regain all their lost powers until all the seals that had confined them had been broken.

Beelzebub roused Kara from her thoughts. "Tell us how you and some of your angel guard learned of the existence of my knights?"

He stared at his globe.

"You are but a speck of dust in the timeline of creation. You couldn't have known about them. I know you didn't discover them on your own, so you must have been informed by a reliable source that had in-depth knowledge of the gods. Only a few possess that knowledge. So, tell me who informed you of their existence?"

Kara pressed her lips together. That information would never come out of her. She'd already caused the death of one oracle. There was no way she was going to endanger the oracle mothers, or any other creatures for that matter. If the archfiends were as clever as the gods like they claimed to be, they would probably guess soon enough. If she could buy the legion some time, she would.

"Who in that pitiful regime you call a *legion* advised you?" asked the archfiend again.

His voice rose in annoyance, and she wondered how long she could keep this up before he smashed her into smithereens. The black veins on his face throbbed as he raised a brow.

"Was it an archangel?" spat the dark god. "Or the one who calls himself *the Chief?*"

A flicker of surprise showed in Kara's face, and the archfiend's eyes narrowed. He had seen it, too. She didn't know how they even knew about Horizon's head guy, but then again Horizon had seen its share of traitors. Her own father had been one.

Kara just shrugged, but she kept her eyes on the archfiend during the whole interrogation. She had to keep him guessing to keep him busy.

Beelzebub's face was unreadable.

"Why go after the knights when the rest of your *kind* are being slaughtered? I'm surprised that you weren't with your precious legion. They could have used a creature like you at the front, even though they are going to lose. You must have been an angel of some importance if they let you go."

His yellow eyes glowed. "What was it you were searching for?"

This inquisition could last forever if she didn't give him something to think about, so Kara kept her face as blank as she could.

"We weren't searching for anything," she said. "We were just doing our duty as guardians. You know, saving mortal lives, the lives you want to destroy."

The archfiend laughed a terrible wicked laugh. But when he spoke again there was no trace of laughter.

"Are there more plans to try and stop my knights? Tell me! It's very important."

Kara raised her brows.

"I'm sure it is, but I don't know what you're talking about. I'm just a guardian—or I was—they don't tell me anything."

The commotion of the battle below them grew louder, and the fear in the pit of her chest increased.

Beelzebub leaned forward in his throne. "What do you know of the *seals?*"

Everything relied on her answer.

She suspected the archfiends could read her mind. She didn't have a plan—not yet. First she needed to free her bonds. Her eyes moved to the death blade that hung around Salthazar's belt.

"Seals? The water animals that live near the ocean?" said Kara, looking back at the giant man sitting on his throne. Her voice steady. She hoped it was a good enough lie.

"I can taste your lies," said Beelzebub. "Somehow the legion discovered the connection between the seals and the knights. This is why you thought you could stop them. But you cannot stop this."

He paused and then added, "Mors vincit omnia."

Kara made a face. "Sorry, my Latin's a little rusty."

"It means *Death conquers all.*"

"And life will go on," countered Kara, slightly pleased at herself.

"Life?" laughed the archfiend. "Your idea of life will not exist after the apocalypse. There will be no more mortal souls for the legion to save because there will be *no more* legion, no more Horizon. Only the dark gods and those who serve us will survive. As much as I appreciate your determination, your will to fight for what you believe is right, it will all be in vain. Horizon's actions are fruitless. Angel kin cannot stop us. You cannot stop a *god*."

Kara didn't know what possessed her, but she couldn't help it.

"You're *not* a god—"

Whack.

Salthazar smacked her on her head, and she staggered forward. After she blinked the white spots from her eyes, she stared at him. His face was stone cold, but his eyes were saying, *Play the game, stupid, for both our sakes.*

Whatever game she decided to play would be her *own* game.

The screams rose from below the cliffs, and she could definitely hear some sort of battle cry, but it was too far away to make it out. Suddenly all the archfiends except Beelzebub stood up. Beelzebub's eyes lingered on her as though he was waiting for something.

The archfiends passed her without a glance in her direction and moved to the edge of the platform. They spread their great big wings, dove down from the edge and disappeared.

Kara shuffled a few curious feet toward the spot where the archfiends had disappeared, but Salthazar grabbed her by the arm and pulled her back forcefully.

She scowled at him, and he smiled back.

"And I thought you liked me," she said.

"Oh, but I do like you," he purred. "Very, very much."

She raised her bonds. "Then prove it and cut these off."

"She's like a stubborn mule that we need to break," said Betaazu before Salthazar could answer her.

Kara looked over to the dais. It was the first time she had seen a real smile on the archfiend's face, and it was terrifying.

Beelzebub raised a finger. "*Break* her."

A very happy Betaazu and two other fiends came at her with whips and chains.

Why hadn't she noticed their weapons before she opened her big stupid mouth?

Kara lifted her hands again.

"Not really fair, is it."

She turned to the Salthazar, "Can you at least untie me?"

But the demon lord's face was a blank mask. He stepped away from her and gave the fiends the space they needed to beat her.

"Thanks," she grumbled. "You hurt my feelings."

At first she had wanted to die. But the look of their weapons and the grins on the fiends' faces sickened her, and her ideas changed. She would fight them with everything she had.

Kara braced herself for the first assault.

The female fiend came at her swinging a chain like a lasso, twirling it at her side and then above her head.

"Show off." Kara snarled. She wished she could use her wings to cut off her head.

The fiend grinned with pointy teeth. "You're mine now, girlie girl. I can't wait to taste you—"

The red-haired fiend came for her, fast and slippery, like a wraith. She swung the chain at Kara's neck.

Kara ducked and heard the chain whip over her head.

Where were the other two fiends?

She heard the second whip before she saw it. It wrapped around her neck and yanked.

The world tilted and Kara heard a crunch as her jaw hit the ground. She opened her mouth and spit out some of her teeth. She had loved her straight teeth, but she needed to control her outraged vanity and save herself. She twisted the chain around her legs and pulled. The force was enough to loosen the chain's grip around her neck. Kara jumped to her feet and glared at the redheaded freak.

She spit out one last tooth. "I'll kill you for this."

Faster than a blink of an eye, there was crack, and the red-haired fiend had wrapped the chain around her ankle. Kara crashed to the ground again. The fiend was on top of her instantly, with her black fangs poised over Kara's neck. Kara bucked and thrashed and kicked the fiend's head with her boot. She rolled over to the side and loosed the chain from her ankle.

The fiend came at her again, fangs exposed.

Kara head butted her with all her strength, and the fiend staggered and fell backward. Without a second to lose, Kara grabbed the chain as best she could with her bound hands and wrapped it around the creature's neck. She pulled and pulled until she felt her arms burning. The fiend finally stopped struggling and was still.

Something hit Kara in her wings and lower back. She fell to her knees. Betaazu stepped over the unconscious female fiend and made his way closer to her. She turned and saw that the other male fiend had crept up behind her as well.

He kicked her in the face, and Kara went sprawling on the ground. As she rolled to a stop, she felt her darkness fed on her anger. She was going to kill them.

The new, cold energy throbbed through her body, and she jumped up and faced the moron that had kicked her in the face. A long, sharp whip dangled from his right hand.

She glanced over to the archfiend and was surprised to see a mix of excitement and anticipation in his face. It was like she had been performing for him, and he was enjoying it immensely. He looked like he was expecting something to happen. She was sure of it.

But what?

The fiend with the whip gave her a cold and calculated smile. In the gloom, his blond hair looked sickly and green. If he wanted a fight, he would get one.

With a crack, the whip sailed toward Kara, and she jumped to the side. But as she regained her balance, the whip flew at her and wrapped around her knees. She screamed as the whip burned through her pants and her skin, as though it had been coated with acid. The fiend yanked his whip, and Kara slammed back onto the ground.

She blinked the spots from her eyes. Her legs were on fire.

"Kneel before your gods!" said the blond fiend. "Swear your loyalty to your new masters, filthy creature."

Kara rolled onto her stomach and spit the hair from her mouth. "Never. You're going to have to kill me, *demon*."

The fiend snarled and pulled on his whip with tremendous strength. Kara soared into the air and came crashing down next to Salthazar. She could see that Salthazar didn't care if they were hurting her. He merely looked annoyed that she might be ruining his chances of making a favorable impression with the archfiends.

She kicked out at Salthazar's legs, and as he fell she snatched his death blade.

She didn't have time to wonder why the blade didn't scorch her fingers as it should have, and she began frantically to saw at her bonds. But before she could make much progress, she was booted in the back and lost her grip of the death blade.

Had her cut been deep enough?

Kara rolled on the ground and flipped onto her knees. The blond fiend loomed over her. His fangs gleamed in the soft light, and his black cloak billowed around him.

"Kneel, girl, or I'll rip your wings from your body."

"I'd like to see you try," snarled Kara.

As the darkness bubbled inside her body, her senses sharpened, and she felt the presence of the thousands who were dead and dying close by. Although she hated the smell of death, she also thrived on its cold, empty feeling. It gave her the strength she needed, and she ripped her bonds apart and tossed them at the fiend.

He shot at her so fast Kara could have sworn he was flying. But her hands were free now, and she was waiting for him. She grabbed his burning whip with both hands and yanked the fiend toward her. As he stumbled forward, she kicked him in the face with all she had. She let go of the whip as he crashed to the ground. Her black veined hands were covered in blisters.

The fiend spit black blood from his mouth as he stood up.

"You're going to pay for this."

"Thought you'd say that." Kara threw her hands behind her and tried to free her wings.

If she could fly, she could get the heck out of there and look for the fourth knight. It was their only chance.

Desperately, she tugged and yanked, but the bonds on her wings were too strong for her raw hands. Even with her super-darkness strength, the bonds wouldn't come off. She was going to have to use something other than her strength. She would have to outsmart it.

The fiend sent his whip sailing toward her neck again, but she spun around and dodged the scorching weapon. Without skipping a beat, she grabbed the whip again, and using his own momentum, she wrapped it around his neck and strangled him with his own weapon. There was a sickening *crack*, and he crumpled to the floor. Black blood sprayed onto her face as his decapitated head thudded onto the ground beside his body.

"Now you've done it." Betaazu came striding across the floor, his face livid. "You stupid, foolish girl."

Kara stepped away from the body, hiding her surprise at what she had done.

"I was wondering when you'd show up."

His savage rage was frightening. He tossed his whip aside and came at her. His black teeth were bared, and his face was contorted in an anger that destroyed any handsome features that he might once have possessed.

Kara raised her brows. "So it's going to be a fair fight, then? Super."

But it wasn't. Not really.

Betaazu shot at her faster than a blink of an eye. He smashed her face with his fist, and she saw stars.

She didn't know what he was doing until the searing pain found her. She screamed like she'd never screamed before. The fiend tugged and tore at her back until he ripped off one of her wings with his bare hands, and she collapsed to the floor.

She lay in a puddle of her own black blood. The world around her spun, and the excruciating pain immobilized her. Scorching, white-hot pain gushed down her back like hot wax. She couldn't think. She couldn't move. She only knew pain.

She heard Betaazu's voice.

"You shouldn't have killed my brother! What were you thinking? You stupid, stupid, girl. Do you even know what you've done? And now look at you. Pathetic. You should have kneeled when we told you to."

He kicked her severed wing, and it slid across the ground, dead. "Now you're broken."

Her mouth was dry, and her throat was raw from screaming. The blood was still running down her back. She wanted to curse him, but she couldn't find the strength to utter a single word. He kicked her hard in the stomach, and she rolled over to the edge of the stone platform.

"You're lucky we need you," hissed Betaazu. "Otherwise I'd kick you off this ledge right now and watch you die a slow and painful death. But not before I tear off your other wing."

With her body trembling in anguish, she had only the strength left to lift up her head. She was close enough to the edge of the stone platform to see the commotion below.

She blinked, and as the scene below her came into focus, Kara felt no more pain and forgot about her severed wing and the dark gods.

There was only the terrifying scene below her.

A colossal battle was being fought in the vast desert below the great volcanic mountain on which she lay. It was monstrous battle between the fiends, demons, and terrors of the Netherworld and the angels.

And the angels were losing.

CHAPTER 18

THE FINAL STAGES

Kara had never seen so many angels together at the same time. There must have been hundreds of thousands of them fighting and losing on the plain below.

As small as mice, they peppered the land like a rippling sea of moving figures. Hundreds of different legions fought the demon platoons. Even from a distance, she could clearly see the large and towering archangels as they fought alongside the smaller angels. They were strong and impressive, but they weren't enough.

The clash of metal and the shrieks of dying angels rose above the plain of battle. The reek of demon and angel blood was a sour, disturbing odor. Hordes of giant monsters and worms and insect-like beasts tore at the bodies of wounded angels like they were paper.

She could see that the legions of angels fought with agility and deathly expertise as they delivered their fatal blows. But when the demons should have stayed down, when the angels should have been tearing the demons' legions apart—the demons kept fighting.

Demons with fatal wounds fought on as if they didn't notice their missing limbs or loss of blood. The demons and other Netherworld creatures fought as though they had some supernatural power.

And then she saw it.

Six archfiends stood in a circle on the outskirts of the battlefield. Thousands of thin, rippling black tendrils of shadow poured out of their arms and wings and shot out over the battle and into the demons and the fiends. The dark power of the archfiends was supplementing the demons with the unnatural strength of the gods.

The angels were outmatched. They could never defeat creatures with an endless supply of impossible power.

Kara's chest stiffened, if only she could have stopped the last knight…

"Enjoying the view?" laughed Betaazu. "Enjoying watching your people die?"

"Shut up."

Kara scouted the vast area for faces she could recognize, but they were too far away and were no larger than ink dots.

Were her friends down there somewhere? Where was David?

The thought of David getting hurt sent a dark ripple coursing through her body. She shook, not from the pain Betaazu had inflicted on her by tearing off her wing, but in anticipation of the pain she would inflict on him later. He was going to pay.

Kara felt more cold and empty inside than she'd ever felt before. Metatron had assigned her friends back onto the field. She knew that they would be down there fighting if they were *still* alive.

She had to do something. The angels would only last another few hours at the rate they were losing. She couldn't stay up here, safe, while her friends and the rest of the legion were fighting.

Why was she up here anyway? Why hadn't they killed her already? Were they going to toy with her, torment her, make her watch the battle until the archfiends won?

Betaazu kicked a pebble down the steep ravine. "Well, they're not *your* people anymore, and soon it won't matter anyway."

Kara gritted her teeth. "They'll always be *my* people."

Could she fly with only one wing?

She was so close.

If she let herself slip off the ledge, would her lonely wing be enough to glide her down to the battle? Would it even open?

Discreetly, she tested her right wing and moved it. It worked.

She slid an inch forward—

"Get her up. It's time," boomed the archfiend's voice behind her.

If she was going to do something, she had to do it now.

It was now or never.

Kara reached down deep into her soul, and with a last strain of strength she gripped the rock and hauled herself toward the ledge—

But something grabbed her neck and pulled her back up.

"Where do you think you're going?" laughed Betaazu.

He heaved her back onto the rocky surface. His face was all smiles, but she could see his surprise in his cat-like eyes. He hadn't thought that she'd risk throwing herself over the edge.

"Thought I'd join the party down there." Kara glared at him. "I'm no use to you. Let me die along my own people. You can do that for me, can't you? Just—just let me go. Please."

The fiend squeezed her neck. "Try that again, and I'll rip off your other wing. Don't think I won't."

Kara could see her black blood trailing behind her as Betaazu hauled her back across the opening. He steadied her in front of the archfiend.

He leaned back in his throne with a bored look in his yellow eyes.

"It puzzles me why you haven't changed yet."

The archfiend looked at her lazily, like he was making a comment about the weather.

"Stranger still that your new body is letting you bleed out. I would have expected it to stop the bleeding."

Kara could feel her essence fade away with every drop that escaped her body. She was frail and broken. Cold sweat trickled down her forehead. If Betaazu hadn't been holding her up by the neck, she'd have dropped like a stone.

"It's a mystery, but now irrelevant. It's time for you to join us and take back what is ours."

The archfiend turned his massive head and bellowed.

"Knights. Come. Your creator commands you."

Three great war horses stepped out from the shadows, and the ground trembled beneath Kara's feet. The knights of the apocalypse waited for their master's instructions. She had totally forgotten about them.

"Go! Destroy them all!"

The ancient mountain shook as the great beasts galloped toward the ledge. Famine, Pestilence and War charged too fast for mortal eyes. They jumped off the ledge and disappeared down into the battle, leaving only a trail of black mist.

Within seconds she heard the screams and desperate shouts of dying angels as the knights unleashed their carnage with guttural, bone-grinding growls.

Kara struggled against Betaazu.

"Let go of me!"

She kicked him in the knee as hard as she could, and he let go for an instant before he charged at her furiously again—

"Enough!"

Betaazu backed away, cursing her with his fist raised.

But Kara didn't care. She turned toward the battlefield. There was a massacre going on down there, and she was missing it. She had to get away from here.

"Yes, my knights are the most powerful warriors in all the worlds," said the archfiend.

Kara turned to look at him, and he mistook her worried frown for interest for his creatures.

He smiled at her, and his eyes gleamed.

"As mighty as they might be, still they are nothing compared to my most precious and most feared possession."

"When Death arrives," his grin widened, "nothing in all the worlds will be able stop him. Nothing. Death is the most powerful and sublime of my dark forces. He is indestructible. The dark gods will reign. The angels will be massacred!"

A faint laugh caught Kara's attention. The redheaded female fiend, her neck swollen and bruised, looked daggers at Kara. All the other fiends were watching her, too, their cat-like eyes gleaming with cold pride.

Kara took a small step back, not from fear of the female fiend, but because she had to get out. And the only way out was down over the ledge.

"It is time, Kara."

Kara turned her attention to the archfiend.

"It's time for what?" she spat.

"It's time to put you to work," said Beelzebub. "It's time for you to embrace what you are and to reveal your true identity. It's time for you to fulfill your destiny."

Kara leaned heavily to her right side because the weight of her right wing pulled her down. Her black blood was smeared all over her clothes and her boots. Her head throbbed again, more intensely. She knew she wouldn't last for very long.

If this was to be her true death, she wanted it to have meaning. She wanted to go out with a bang. But first she needed to find the knight. Nothing else mattered.

Using her injuries as a disguise, she staggered and then took another shuffle backward toward the edge.

"I was always destined to be a guardian angel," Kara winced at the pain in her head. "Of that I am *sure*. No, I *know* it."

Beelzebub admired her calmly. It infuriated her.

"You were destined to become something far greater than merely an angel or a demon. Your father knew it too."

Kara rubbed her throbbing head.

What was he talking about? He clearly enjoyed hearing himself speak. Good. Let him talk.

She took another step back and shifted her weight so that she could make a run, or rather a shuffle, for the edge.

"But your father was a fool, a selfish demon fool. In his own quest to acquire greatness and power for himself, he failed to see your real potential, your *real* destiny. He was blinded by his selfishness and failed to learn the *real* truth, the *real* secret about where you came from. About *your* bloodline."

Bloodline?

Kara felt a cold surge of darkness rise inside her soul. The darkness was trying to snuff out the tiny light that was the only part of her that was still *her*. She was able to push the darkness down for now, but she knew she wasn't strong enough anymore. Soon it would take over, and she would lose control.

Her head pounded, wetness dripped from her nose, and when she wiped it, her hand was stained with black blood. She had to move.

"Your headaches are just a sign that the transformation is nearly complete," said the archfiend as if he read her mind.

He paused for a moment, pleased that he had intrigued her.

"It is an end…but also a new beginning."

Kara had no idea what he was mumbling about. She focused on her weakening knees and throbbing head. She didn't have time to listen to these psychotic archfiends.

She took another discreet step back.

The archfiend smiled evilly. "You are ready now."

He stretched out a large hand in front of her.

"Come, join me, and I promise your headaches will end."

There was no way in Horizon Kara was going to *join* him. She couldn't take it anymore, couldn't take the lies, the self-important monsters, her hammering headaches—so she spun around and shuffled away as fast as her weakened body would allow.

She saw the lip of the ledge and heard the heavy pounding of boots behind her. He was too close. She halted and whirled around, the heels of her feet dangling over the ledge.

"Stop or I jump!"

Betaazu skidded to a stop, just a step away from her. She could see the fury blazing in his eyes. His teeth were bared like he wanted to rip out her neck.

"Stand down, Betaazu," said the archfiend, still in that insufferable, lazy tone.

He looked at Kara for a moment. "Why do you even still care for them? There is no hope for them."

She stared at her ring.

215

"There's *still* hope," she muttered more to herself than to them. She saw Betaazu stare at her ring, but his expression was blank.

The dark god laughed. "Hope! There is no more hope, well, not for the angels or the mortals. It is over for them."

"Come to me now," he ordered.

"But there is." Kara turned to the archfiend. "There is still hope. Because there's still a seal that's holding on—"

"No, there isn't."

"Yes there is." She lifted her hand, and her golden ring glimmered in the light.

"This ring tells me that there is."

Painfully, she steadied herself with her right wing and prayed it could keep her in one piece until she jumped off the ledge.

"There's always hope," she said.

"I'm going after the last knight, and you can't stop me. I'm going to kill it."

Just as she was about to whirl around and jump, she stopped, not because she was afraid of splattering herself at the bottom, but because something wasn't quite right about the way they were looking at her. She was more like an injured bird than anything else. They should be furious, but instead they were pleased. *Why?*

She was being stupid. *Who cares what they thought.* What mattered was finding the knight while there was still hope.

"I will find him," she said defiantly as she prepared to jump.

Beelzebub stood up from his throne and said, "You already have."

Kara scanned the chamber and then looked back at the archfiend. She made a face.

"You? You're the fourth knight?"

Beelzebub smiled, his eyes widened.

"Of course not. Kara Nightingale, of the legion of angels, *you* are. You are Death."

CHAPTER 19

DEATH

Kara nearly fell over the ledge.

Impossible. She took one careful step forward, all the while keeping her eyes on the archfiend. She waited for him to start laughing or for any sign or twitch in his face that would give away his lies. But his face was stone cold, blank.

Betaazu kept his distance, but she was aware that he could grasp her in an instant.

Whatever was going on, she was not free yet.

The archfiend was mocking her. It couldn't be true.

"Is that the best you can do?" she said finally. "You sound really desperate and really, really delusional. No, I take that back—it's pathetic. I'm not a knight."

She forced a laugh. "Where's my horse? I don't even know *how* to ride a horse. This is crazy. I don't even know why I'm wasting my time speaking to you."

"Because you know it's true." The dark god's voice was cool and calculating. His smirk widened.

Kara felt a tiny spark of fear, but spoke with conviction.

"No, I don't! How can I? I thought you people were supposed to be *all knowing*? But you're not the brightest, are you? So let me clarify this to you. *You* didn't *make* me. I didn't sprout from the ground from some otherworldly bog of eternal darkness. I exist. I exist in this body because I'm an angel—"

Their laugher set her fury boiling. If she'd had the use of her other wing, she would have ripped the smiles off their faces, especially the redhead.

"Whatever I am," Kara's voice wavered. "Whatever *monster* or creature you made of me …it doesn't matter, because I know I'm *not* a knight, because I'm *still* me. I'm still the same girl inside, and you can't change that no matter how hard you try. Your scheme hasn't worked."

The archfiend stared at her for a few moments.

"Oh, but it did work. And that *girl* you claim to be inside, well, you won't be for much longer."

Kara forced a laugh. "That's bull. You know it, and I know it."

"I do not know what *bull* is, but I can guarantee that the last of that angel dust that still flickers in you will waste away in a few minutes' time."

The archfiend paused and then added, "No, I take that back, in a few seconds. In a few seconds, you will no longer remember what it was like to be an angel. You will not remember the legion, Horizon, or your friends. You will not remember who you were before the change. You'll only know what you have become. You are the fourth knight."

"I'm not." Kara shook her head like a stubborn child.

She was still bleeding a lot. She stood in a puddle of her black blood. She tried not to think about it too much because the more she dwelled on the blood, the more she felt the effect of it. It was getting harder and harder to remain standing. She faltered slightly, and she saw that the dark god had seen her falter, too.

"You see," he said pleased, too pleased. "Stop fighting it and let go. Embrace the darkness and all its purity. Let go of the foul angel and become the creature feared by all. Become Death."

Kara was so angry and tired that she could hardly think or stand. Her head hurt so much that she thought her brain had melted. Her eyes narrowed to slits.

"I think there's been enough death, don't you agree?" said Kara. "I won't be part of your schemes."

She gritted her teeth at the burning pain that shot down her body. Her vision blurred, and the archfiend became two instead of one. She shook her head, but it made the pounding worse. She could see Betaazu smiling at her pain. How she hated him. How she hated them all.

She knew she should jump now, but something was still holding her back.

"I'm going to get better," she croaked.

Her throat was raw and was closing up. She tried to convince herself that she was all right by speaking again. "You're lying. You're a liar. You're just trying to trick me."

"Am I?" laughed the dark god. "You can feel it, can't you? In the pit of your pitiful little angel soul, you feel it pushing its way in. It wants to show itself. You want it to come. You know I speak the truth, *Death*."

Kara trembled, "Don't call me that."

"Why not? It is your *true* name."

Could it really be true?

"It is true," said the archfiend, as though he was reading her mind again.

"Why do you think we injected you with the extract of darkness? Because we knew. We knew if we combined the extract with your special essence, your unique bloodline, we could create the final knight. You are the warrior of the dark gods, the killer of angels. You are the final seal."

"Your bloodline has been traced back to the beginning of all things, to the very first archfiends, before we were cast into prison by the archangels."

Beelzebub sat back down on his throne. "And when rumors of a special angel with the powers of both an angel and an elemental reached us in our remote *doomed* prison, we knew. We waited eons for you, for this chance. You—and you alone—were the missing link. Without you, we could never have broken free from our *perpetual* doom."

221

Kara's eyes widened. "No, it can't be."

"Believe it," said Betaazu. "This," he raised his arms, "is all your doing. You helped release our masters. You did this. You saved us all."

"No." Kara shook her head.

Black blood dripped from her nose and from the hole in her back. Her headache pulsed unmercifully.

"Yes," said the archfiend, confident of his ancient intelligence. "The darkness thrives inside you, and you will destroy the archangels, the angels, and all living things. Rejoice in darkness. It is eternal. You are perfect."

The world shifted around Kara. Images that the white oracle had spoken played inside her mind. She could see the shadowy figure with great wings that soared through the blackened and smoky sky. The white oracle had shown her images of death, the fourth knight of the apocalypse. And she was *it*.

"But I thought…" She shook her head. *What did she think? What else could the wings have meant other than that she was becoming a monster freak, a killer of angels?* But to think that she was going to change into *the* ultimate monster was too much to bear.

But what about her light…the light that still lingered somewhere in her soul?

"I won't change," said Kara. Her voice wavered, but she didn't care. "It's not going to happen."

"You *will* change. It's inevitable." The archfiend spoke confidently.

222

"Your defiance is a strength that will make you an even better knight, a better bringer of death."

"I won't," Kara repeated. Her voice was stronger.

"You said it yourself. I didn't change yet, so it's not working. Whatever you did to me, didn't work. You failed."

A cold smile spread on the archfiend's face. "No, I didn't."

She wouldn't accept this defeat. She'd known and tasted fear and pain before, but it was nothing compared to what went through her now.

"NO!" she screamed, enraged because she knew it was true.

Kara stumbled toward his throne, limbs wobbling. She fumbled in a fog with her broken body.

Kill him. Kill the monster creator. It was all she could think of. Her steps became more feeble, and her vision blurred.

She would kill him, if it were the last thing she did.

The archfiend smirked. "And now, my dear, it's time to give you a little push—"

As Kara neared the dais, the dark god raised his hand and shot a black tendril of power straight into Kara's chest.

It was like being shot by a twelve-gauge shotgun. She was blasted to the ground in a flash of blinding pain. The darkness overwhelmed her like a hot fever, and an uncontrollable and ancient evil welled up inside her. Dark fire was dragging her down into an abyss. She was losing her hold of the light. She was losing herself. She was losing Kara.

Her golden ring shimmered, but then the color faded, and it became black. The little light inside her flickered one last time and went out.

A moment passed and then the creature she had become jumped to its feet.

It felt no more pain. It felt nothing. But its senses were heightened, and it could see everything. It knew everything. It smelled the terror. It smelled the blood of mortals and angels. It tasted the pain of millions. It licked its gray lips. It wanted to kill. It was created to kill. It wanted to extinguish the light. It wanted only darkness. It understood darkness. It *was* darkness.

A faint, red-gray mist covered its body, and red veins began to grow in its glossy gray skin. Long black hair billowed from its head, and where a wound had been moments ago, a perfect large black leathery wing sprouted and grew.

The creature turned and awaited its master's instructions. It wanted to please its master.

"Kill the archangels," its master ordered. "Them first. Then kill all the angels. Leave not a single one."

The creature sneered in delight. It wouldn't fail. It longed to taste the death of the angels. It licked its gray lips in anticipation and spread its massive veiny wings.

With a dripping maw, Death smiled, jumped from the ledge, and dove down into the battle.

CHAPTER 20
DAVID

David swung and sliced off the head of a clown demon with his soul blade. It hissed at him before it thumped to the ground with a surprised expression frozen on its face. Black blood sputtered over David's boots as he kicked the body.

"Stupid clown demons," he clenched his jaw.

He would slice all the clown demons to ribbons. He hated clown demons. He remembered that Lilith had changed him into a clown demon, and that he had wanted to hurt Kara. It still haunted him that he could have hurt the only girl in all the worlds that he'd have given his life to protect.

Kara...

The thought of her created an ache in his chest. *Was she all right?*

He remembered how unbelievably *attracted* he'd been to her the first time he'd seen her in Horizon. He had felt on fire even before he knew her name. Her brown eyes had sparkled when she had looked at him, and he had been bewitched. He had never been the same.

Of course she had thought him arrogant, rude, ill mannered, and charming—all of those things, but that had just been his way to break the ice. She made him nervous, and it made him want to be his best around her. No other girl had ever had that effect on him before. She was electrifying.

Movement caught his eye. David spun and thrust his soul blade hilt-deep into the eye socket of a lime-green creature. The demon went limp and sank to the ground.

He wiped the black-green blood from his blade on the sleeve of his jacket and looked up.

Throngs of angels and demons surrounded him on the east side of the vast desert plain. He was in the middle of the hot zone. He fought alongside a battalion of a thousand angels. And even though the angels were outnumbered by demons that kept on coming at them as if they were sprouting from the ground, the angels were skilled fighters, and the demons were falling fast. Their bodies crumbled into ashes that blew away in the wind or disappeared into the earth.

They could win this. They would win this war.

Unlike the other angels, it came as no surprise to David when they found a demon and monster cavalry waiting when his legion had arrived at the foot of the volcano. Mr. Patterson had predicted it. He had told them to expect the archfiends. And they were here.

The war had started in the blink of an eye.

The wails of the dead and dying mixed with the clatter of metal on metal and the thumping of fists on flesh. It felt as though the earth were cracking like an egg. The crescendo of sounds was so continuous that they all merged into a single annihilating roar. The ground trembled and thundered like the beating of a giant heart.

David had never been in a war of this magnitude. All he could do was take cover and get his bearings. He fought like a good soldier. He fought for what was right. He fought for the freedom of Earth and of Horizon.

He fought for Kara.

He struck both his soul blades into the abdomen of a zombie demon, pulled them out, and made his way forward into the melee. Dust and sand obscured the flailing arms and weapons so that it was hard to tell angel from demon.

But his more pressing problem was Kara.

He was faltering because he was distracted. He couldn't stop thinking about Kara and where she was. He knew she had flown off to search for the last knights. But now that Jenny's ring had gone, it was all up to Kara.

Kara, where were you?

He should be with her.

He saw a flash of purple and spotted Jenny right away. Her purple hair and jacket were like a beacon, and he knew it wasn't such a good idea to stick out so much. He fought his way near her.

227

She wore her silver bow wrapped around her back, and like him she brandished a soul blade in each hand. She slithered like a snake behind an unsuspecting demon, and with a flick of her wrists she perforated the demon's neck, and it slumped to the ground.

David had forgotten how skilled Jenny was with a blade. He'd always thought of her as an archer, but she didn't have enough time to nock her arrows here. There were too many demons, and she didn't have enough arrows. She would have needed thousands of them.

David scanned the battle. He recognized a few faces, but Peter and Ashley were nowhere in sight. He prayed they were all right.

Jenny caught sight of David, but she didn't smile at him as he rushed over to her. Even before he reached her, he knew something was wrong. Her face was taunt and troubled. She kept opening and closing her hands.

"I'm glad to see you in one piece," she said.

Her face and clothes were stained in black blood. "Any news from Kara?"

David shrugged and didn't meet Jenny's eyes. "Not yet."

"David, I've got some bad news," she said quickly, looking over her shoulder.

He read the panic in her voice, and his own cold panic started to well inside him. He already knew what she was going to say.

"My—my ring's gone."

She looked terrified. "It just…it just disappeared, just like that. I didn't even realize. It could have happened hours ago. I had forgotten about it."

And then she spoke quickly. "What does it mean? Do you think anything happened to Kara? Do you think she's still okay?"

David couldn't answer her because he didn't know. He didn't want to face the obvious explanation—that Kara had failed.

Jenny quickly changed the subject.

"Never seen so many demons in all my angel days. I don't know what I expected. Who knew there would be so many demons in the Netherworld?"

"I knew there'd be lots of them, but it appears that they all came out to play today."

A demon loomed over behind Jenny, but before she noticed it, David knocked it on its head with the pommel of his dagger and sliced its neck as it collapsed to the ground.

Jenny looked mildly surprised. "Thanks."

"Don't mention it. Won't be the last time, that's for sure."

David knew she was looking for someone special.

"Did you see Peter anywhere?" said Jenny, as though she were reading his mind.

David shook his head sadly.

"No. But I'm sure he's okay. He's a real fighter, our Pete. And I'm sure he's got all kinds of new tricks and gadgets up his sleeve. I wouldn't worry about him."

But Jenny didn't look relieved. She looked worried.

"He'll be fine, Jen," said David. "I promise."

"Don't make promises you can't keep."

David thought that she was about to cry, but whatever frustration she felt inside she vented on a demon who had no idea what had hit him until her blade had perforated its head.

"I don't know, David. There're so many of them." Jenny straightened up.

"With the rings gone…with Kara gone…"

She faltered, her voice cracked.

"Don't say it, Jenny," said David.

"Maybe our rings are gone, but that doesn't mean Kara's is. There's still one knight left, and she still has a chance at killing it. I know she can do this. I have to believe she can, and she *will*. It's up to us to give her all the time we can. It's our job to make sure we kill as many demons as we can."

"Do you really think we can beat them?"

It was hard to tell.

"It's not a question of *if* anymore. In fact, it's not a question at all. We just *have* to."

"What about Metatron's plans?"

David spotted a higher demon making its way slowly toward them. It meandered toward them like it didn't think they posed any real threat.

"What about Metatron?" David's blades twitched in his hands.

"Well, did you hear anything about them? About how he's planning to destroy the archfiends and win this thing? David? There's something behind me, isn't there—?"

The higher demon pulled out a death blade faster than a flash of light, but David was already moving.

He knocked the death blade with his own weapon and slammed into the surprised higher demon. They both went down in a cloud of dust. David caught a glimpse of its laughing face, and a wildness spread in him. His blades flashed, and then there was a squish of metal in flesh and a crunch of bone. Black blood sprayed from the demon's severed neck, and David slammed his other blade down into the demon's head. The higher demon went limp, and David jumped up, pumped with adrenaline.

"I don't know anything about Metatron's plans," said David. "It's not like the guy trusts me or anything. I'd doubt he'd even tell me his brand of cigars. I'm just another grunt to him."

"I think we're all grunts to that guy."

Jenny kicked a small imp in the face and sliced his throat before he could run off. The creature fell.

"I just don't see how we're going to win this war. We're seriously out numbered."

David knew Jenny was right. He had done the math, too. The demons outnumbered the legion twenty to one. It was crazy.

Suddenly, the ground trembled and moaned like the roar of a hundred thunderstorms. An explosion of earth and dust created a giant cloud, and hundreds of severed demon limbs and bodies fell to the ground around them.

"What in the souls was that?"

David cocked his head toward the dust cloud.

"I guess we've got our answer."

The cloud dissipated, and Metatron stood in the middle of a small crater with a devious smile on his face. There was not a speck of dust on his suit. His female entourage danced around him, cutting down any demons that had survived the blast.

David smiled impishly. "He's a jerk, I'll admit that. But you can't deny the man's got some serious moves."

Jenny rolled her eyes, drew her sword quickly, and perforated the neck of a goblin-like demon.

"Oh please. We've all got moves. All he has is a bad haircut and oily skin."

They both burst out laughing, a strange sound amongst the wails of the dying. But all too soon, their little burst of hope died.

Cries erupted like wind, and David thought it was another one of Metatron's homemade bombs. But what he saw sent a cold shiver through his body.

The dead demons' bodies began to twist and move. They began mending themselves and stitching their limbs and heads together until they were whole again. The only signs that they had been dead were the semi-dried stains of blood on their bodies. Otherwise they were as good as new.

"This is not real. It can't be." Jenny's voice came out like a whisper.

"This can't be happening."

David watched horrified, transfixed, as demons that had suffered blows that no otherworldly creature could have survived didn't stay down. They kept getting back up.

"They're not dying," said David, astonished and disgusted at the same time.

"They're different. They're *stronger* somehow."

"This isn't just a regular fight anymore," he said slowly. "We're fighting what won't be killed."

"But how can that be?" Jenny jumped back as one of the imp creatures she had killed a few moments ago, and that technically should have stayed dead, started to screw on its severed head like a plastic doll.

"What's giving them this new strength? How can they stay alive?"

"I don't know."

This was something new. The archfiends had to be responsible.

The angels had fought with all they had, but the demons kept coming. And soon fear spread like a wildfire, and the battalions broke apart. Some angels ran. But most stayed, determined to fight till the end.

Piles of angel bodies accumulated on the ground. The demons cheered, cutting and slicing the already dead angels just for the sick and twisted pleasure of it. And when the angel souls rose from their fallen bodies, the demons ate them savagely. Although they were already drunk on the souls they had ingested, they wanted more.

David felt sick. There was no stopping them.

"Stay together," Metatron commanded.

"Don't run. We must fight! Where are you going! Guardians come back!"

The legions broke apart.

Although a small group of angels protected the big archangel, it wouldn't be enough. A few hundred angels were nothing compared with the tidal wave of unstoppable demons. They wouldn't last more than a few hours. The archfiends were going to win.

They were all going to die.

"David, we have to get out of here!" Jenny sliced off the head of a massive lizard-like demon. But as it hit the ground, tendrils of black mist shot up from the neck stump, grabbed its severed head, and pulled it back on.

"This is so wrong!"

Jenny kicked the creature's head one last time and then jumped over to David.

"David, we can't stay here. They're slaughtering us. We need to leave and regroup. David!"

But David ignored her and didn't move. Even as retreating angels came crashing into his shoulders, he stood still and scanned the area. Jenny shook and pulled him, but her shouts were empty. He was completely preoccupied. He had to find the source of the demons' power. He had to find whatever it was, for Kara.

Something had happened to change things. It was like *something* had started feeding the demons with supernatural power intravenously. Whatever it was, it had to be near. It had to be close. If he could find it and break the connection, then maybe…

Barely aware that Jenny was still trying to get his attention, David watched as Metatron and his legion of angels ploughed through a wall of lesser demons. He was fierce and every great blow sent dozens of broken demons hurtling through the air. But how long could the archangel keep it up? How long could any of them keep this up? Every time a demon went down, they got back up, but the angels' souls were devoured when they fell, and they stayed down. At this rate, it wouldn't matter if they won because the angels were being annihilated.

A new wave of spider-like demons emerged from a hill in the east and scurried over the battlefield toward more unsuspecting angels. The air felt heavy and thick, like a fog had suddenly materialized.

David looked up. Above the battlefield a web of shadows spread like a network of thin strings. He followed the black threads.

Six giant creatures with black wings stood in a circle on the perimeter of the battle.

Even in the distance they were enormous, bigger than archangels, and David knew instantly that these were the archfiends. Black tendrils shot from the fingers of their outstretched arms and spread over the battle like a giant web of dark power. He could see the tendrils moving and pulsing like veins as they supplied the creatures with an endless supply of power.

A shudder went through him, but he knew what he had to do.

"David?" Jenny followed his gaze. "What are those things?"

"Archfiends."

Metatron beat a creature to a bloody puddle nearby.

"Metatron!" David bellowed.

Metatron stopped pounding the creature and looked up. His face was unreadable, and his shades were smeared with green-black blood.

David pointed to the sky with his blade and then to archfiends standing at the edges of the battle. The big man stiffened as he surveyed the webs in the sky above them. He turned back to David, his brows furrowed, and David knew the archangel understood what they needed to do.

Metatron bellowed orders and charged into a gang of lesser demons and imps. With one stroke of his sword, he severed six demons in half, and they fell at his feet. His legion formed two lines on either side of him and slaughtered every creature that came close. They drove the beasts back until there was a clear path through the fallen bodies, a clear path for David.

"Jenny, get ready." David only had only a few moments before the demons reformed. It had to be enough.

"We don't have much time. You're going to have to trust me."

"Get ready for what? What is it that we need to do?"

Jenny stared at the archfiends, almost transfixed by fear.

"We need to break the connection."

"What?"

"Come on, hurry!"

Most the other angels ran in the opposite direction, but with Jenny at his heels, David charged over the path of demon bodies that Metatron had cleared and headed straight toward the great winged archfiends.

CHAPTER 21
FREEDOM RUN

David ran like the devils were at his heels because he knew that they soon would be. He heard Jenny's tread behind him, but he didn't look back. He didn't want to break his momentum and slow down even for a second. He only had a few moments to reach the nearest archfiend.

He could see that it stood at the edge of a cliff just below the volcano. It was female, he was certain of that. A crown glimmered in the gray light on top of her flowing black tresses. Metal armor covered her upper body like a tight bodice, and black veins pulsed under her gray-colored skin. Her beautiful cold features were sculpted and refined, unnaturally perfect. She radiated power. David could feel it all around him. It pushed him back like some sort of force field.

She immediately made him think of Kara. It was obvious now, when he looked at her more closely. The dark gods had infected Kara with a poison that would morph her into something that looked like this great fiend.

He remembered her sadness when she had first showed him the veins that covered her trembling hands. He had felt a cold chill down his spine when they had spread to her face and the rest of her body. He knew she had been terrified she would turn into a monster.

Kara...

David ran harder.

He would make the poison go away. He would find a cure to help her. Something. It was his *job* to protect her. They were soul mates, and he desperately wanted the old Kara back. He'd do anything to make her pain go away. Heck, he would even rip off those cursed wings if he had to. He'd kill all of these wretched archfiends with his bare hands if it meant he could get her back. He would do anything for her.

David sprinted.

Kill them all. He hit the wall of darkness that surrounded the female archfiend like a cold mist and pressed on. He didn't even know if the legion could defeat the archfiends, but he didn't care. He could only hope that Metatron had a lot more of those bombs, or something better. Right now he had more pressing matters.

He had to *break* the connection.

He had to destroy the archfiends' web. It was the only thing he could do to help the angels. It was a long shot. God knows if it would even work. But he would take the chance or die trying.

He wasn't sure what he *was* going to do exactly.

Some of the demons who had been destroyed were already on their feet again. Soon they'd be fighting, and his path would be gone.

He had less than thirty seconds.

He made a wild dash.

Running was the right thing to do, wasn't it?

He was so close now that he could see the wicked smile on the archfiend's face. He was nearly overwhelmed by the smell of death that exuded from her, her unfathomable beauty, and the cold, icy power that she radiated.

The air around him became cool, and a high-pitched ringing began to reverberate in his head. The ringing in his ears worsened with each step, and he couldn't hear Jenny behind him anymore. But he couldn't look back. Not now. He was nearly there. He only hoped she wasn't too far behind. He would need her help.

David was a lot of things, truth be told, but he wasn't a fool. The female thing scared the crap out of him. He didn't want to die, but if his sacrifice helped save Kara, he would do it. He gripped his soul blades in both hands and dashed toward her.

Her yellow cat-like eyes had no kindness in them. If she was surprised to see him, it didn't show on her stone-cold face. She didn't move a centimeter. She didn't even move her head, but she followed him with her eyes. Tendrils of black power poured out of her into the battle, never missing a beat.

Could she multitask?

He didn't wait to find out. Maybe she felt that he wasn't a threat, but merely a tiny little insect.

That would be her mistake.

He didn't aim for her face, or her chest, but hurled his soul blades into the creature's hands.

She winced as dark blood spurted from her outstretched fingers. And then the black tendrils flickered and vanished.

David looked to the sky. Although part of the web shimmered and faded, the shadow branches from the other five archfiends still remained strong. But there was a gap in their web. He had damaged it. And the fact that he actually could make a difference filled him with hope. He had given some of the angels enough time to recover and regroup.

"You did it! You really did it!" Jenny sounded astonished.

David slowed to a jog, impressed by his own perfect aim. It had been *way* too easy.

And then the archfiend turned her head in his direction.

Her yellow eyes bored into his as she inspected him, really inspected him. She smiled a wicked smile that made David freeze. She turned her gaze casually to the blades sticking out of her hands. They were nothing but tiny, annoying splinters. She pulled them out, one by one, and tossed them away.

"Jenny, get back!" cried David. He braced himself and pulled the spare soul blade from his boot. It was coming.

The archfiend appeared to be amused by this annoying little angel. With a flick of her wrists, and before he even had time to blink, she sent a bolt of darkness crashing into him.

Jenny's cry echoed in his ears as he felt the searing pain and was lifted in the air. Then blackness and white-hot pain like he'd never felt before. The smell of death and decaying bodies washed over him and inside him. He felt as though his body had been ripped apart. Another wave of pain hit him, and he went down into the blackness of a bottomless abyss.

The world around him vanished.

Was this death? Was this his true death? If only he could have seen Kara one last time…if only he could have told her how much she meant to him, how much he truly cared…

But then sick inhuman laughter replaced the ringing in his ears, and the pain stopped.

"You wish to die at the hands of a dark god," said a voice looming over him and everywhere at once.

"It is an honorable death. I prefer honorable enemies to ambitious ones, and you have refused to submit. I admire your courage, and so I will grant you a quick death, angel boy."

David slowly got to his feet, amazed that his weapon still hung in his hand. But he made no move toward the archfiend. He let her talk.

"Touch him again, and I will send you back to wherever you came from." Jenny stood behind David with her bowstring taut and three silver arrows nocked and ready.

The archfiend female threw back her head and laughed. "Your weapons cannot hurt me, spirit of the heavens."

She lifted her palms and showed David and Jenny that the wounds on her hands were gone. They had healed themselves.

"I'll take my chances," said Jenny with a fierce grin.

David took a careful step back and whispered. "Jenny, don't be stupid—"

"Yes, please *be* stupid, Jenny," said the archfiend.

"I miss killing things, especially defiant little angel *specks*. How wondrous it feels to be out and killing again, removing the filth from this earth."

"Look who's talking," spat Jenny.

The archfiend didn't lose her smile.

"You angels have always been foolish and insubordinate. You'll never learn. Even after all these years, you still don't know when to admit to weakness and bow down to your gods."

Her beautiful face furrowed. "And then you tricked us and caged us like beasts. Perhaps luck was on your side, and you cunning little specks managed to fool us once. But never again.

"We only wish to repay your kindness. We will destroy this foul little world you cherish so, and we will destroy Horizon and all its creatures."

David caught a glimpse of Metatron sneaking up behind the dark god. He was hiding in a group of dead-but-waking demons, and she hadn't seen him yet.

David suspected that these powerful creatures probably had eyes in the backs of their heads or could sense danger before it hit. He had to keep her focused on him.

"Sorry to disappoint you, giant-woman-person," began David. "But that's not going to happen because we're *going* to stop you."

The archfiend's smile widened, and just as she made to flick her wrists again, Metatron's sword perforated her neck.

Metatron moved so fast that David could hardly follow him. He appeared on the other side of the archfiend and struck another sword in her abdomen, just below her breastplate. The archfiend roared, but when she whirled in anger, Metatron was already gone.

David smiled. He wished he could move that fast.

Metatron stood in front of her now and hurled his short dagger at the archfiend's head.

But faster than humanly or supernaturally possible, she caught his blade easily and tossed it away. With a flick of her wrist, she sent a helix of darkness at the archangel, and he went down entangled in black shadow tendrils. Metatron screamed, and the archfiend spread her wings and landed on the ground next to him. Her face twisted in a mask of fury and hatred.

David sprinted to help Metatron, but something slammed into him and whacked him on the side of the head. David fell to his knees for an instant and blinked the black spots from his eyes. But then he managed to get up and swing his blade into the face of the creature that had knocked him down. It had thick brown leathery skin and a mouth with too many teeth. It hissed at him and staggered back with a large gash exposing raw, wet flesh across its cheek.

As David aimed his dagger, he saw Jenny holding her own against four tree-like monsters with human eyes and gangly roots for limbs.

His dagger flew.

It struck the beast in the neck, and the creature spat up black blood and fell back again with a roar. Vile liquid squirted from the wound in its chest. But it wasn't finished. It pulled out the dagger and licked the blood from it.

"Nice," said David, only too aware that it was about to attack again.

A scream, a bone-chilling scream interrupted him.

Metatron.

He was convulsing on the ground with the archfiend looming over him and shooting tendrils of death into him again and again. She had a terrifying smile of her face.

Metatron screamed one last time, and then nothing. He stopped moving.

Panic filled David. He didn't know if the archangel was dead or if the female archfiend had merely disabled him, but staring at the indestructible Metatron face down on the ground caused David to swallow his shout.

And then Metatron's legions came out of nowhere and threw themselves at the archfiend, swords and daggers flying. But she was waiting for them.

She flicked her wrist, and a flash of black tendrils came hurtling toward the angels and blasted them into dust.

"You beast! You monster!" Jenny's cry rang in David's ears.

He stared at the lingering particles of dust. The archfiend could have easily killed him like it did the others.

Why hadn't it done that?

He had an overwhelming feeling that it was waiting for something.

Something black soared above the battlefield. It was smaller than the other six fiends, but it poured a blackness over the retreating angels that incinerated them until there was nothing left but puffs of falling ash. The creature banked suddenly and headed toward them.

Jenny pointed behind him.

"David, that's another one of those archfiend beasts. It's coming right at us. If we don't leave now, we won't make it!"

David looked around. Netherworld monsters had overwhelmed the field like a plague. There were no signs of angels anywhere.

Had they all gone? Had they all been destroyed so quickly? Did they all flee?

He turned back to the flying archfiend.

David couldn't explain it, but this new archfiend was different. It didn't wear the metal armor, and he could tell it was female. He had a strange feeling that the creature was familiar. "David, let's go!" barked Jenny. She leapt backward.

The black winged demon flapped toward them and then dove straight for David.

It moved so fast that David only saw a black blur of wings.

He whirled, striking out before he could get a good look at the creature. He glimpsed only a flash of withered gray skin and jagged pointy teeth before he sliced his soul blades across its chest.

It screamed like nothing he had ever heard before. The ragged cloth on its chest ripped open and revealed a bony misshapen chest covered in red veins. The creature's yellow eyes blazed in fury as it slammed a clawed hand into David's face.

Although pain ripped through his cheek, he couldn't take his eyes off the creature.

It had Kara's face.

CHAPTER 22

THE FOURTH KNIGHT

David felt the world shifting around him. The dark gods were playing a cruel joke on him because what he saw was impossible.

"Kara?" he breathed, staring into the face of a memory of the girl he loved.

The creature snarled with blackened pointy teeth. There was no recognition in its yellow eyes, only death—death and fury. And yet, it had Kara's face.

David shook his head.

The beautiful girl with chestnut brown hair and dazzling brown eyes that he had once known had become a winged creature with claws and dull gray skin. Its long black hair dripped with black liquid. It still wore Kara's clothes and her boots, although they were torn and covered in filth. It was as though she had tried to rip them off when she had transformed, to destroy what she used to be.

"Holy souls," said Jenny peering from behind him. "David, what happened to her?"

David threw an arm up and pushed Jenny back.

"I don't know. I think—I think this is what the oracles saw. What they made her see. The change, the transformation."

He looked at the creature solemnly. "This is what Kara had feared she was going to become...become a..."

Monster.

But David couldn't utter the words. It was too painful.

Did she or it recognize him at all? Was there a little part of Kara that still existed in that thing?

There had to be. He wouldn't let himself feel the dread that threatened to take him over.

Kara had to be in there somewhere.

"What did you do to her!" barked Jenny as she sprang forward, but David held her back.

"Kara?" he asked and took a careful step forward. He dared not take his eyes off the creature. He had forgotten about the all the demons, the archfiends, and the war. There was only him and the creature, Kara.

"It's me, David."

The creature blinked.

He lifted his hands in surrender, his voice calm, only his lips trembled.

"You know me. We're friends remember? Well, we're more than friends. Don't you recognize me?"

The creature tucked in its wings and sank back on its thighs, waiting for a chance to pounce.

David's throat tightened, but he forced down his fears.

"Kara. I know you're still in there somewhere. It's me, David."

He forced himself to look straight into the creature's eyes, but he saw nothing, nothing but a dark hunger.

"Kara. Come back to me. Fight it. Fight it, Kara. You're the strongest guardian I know. The strongest in all the legion. You can do this—"

The archfiend landed beside Kara and smiled at the horror on their faces.

"There is no more Kara."

"This creature is no longer your angel friend. In fact, there is no more angel in her at all. She has become a creature of darkness, a mutation of wild and dark power. She is marvelous."

The archfiend's eyes were wide with superiority. "She has become *Death*."

The creature turned at the sound of its name, acknowledging its master, and David thought he was going to be sick.

"The fourth and final knight of the apocalypse," continued the archfiend. "She is our most deadly weapon. You angel specks should have yielded to our higher power. But you refused to bow down to us. Now it's time for you to taste the wrath of a dark god. Kill them! Kill the angels! Kill them all!"

Death sprang.

David had only the time to knock Jenny out of the way as the creature slammed into him, claws ripping at his face. He had his

249

blade in his hands, but he didn't use it. He couldn't bring himself to hurt her. He believed that Kara was still in there.

He managed to pin the creature's hands together and kick her off him, but the creature hovered overhead and then dove again. Only this time it went for Jenny.

"No!" David ran after it cursing.

"Here, here! It's me you want. Leave her alone!"

Jenny held her blade with shaking hands.

"Kara, no please. It's Jen," she pleaded. "I'm your friend—"

But Death dove straight for her, knocked her blade out of her hands, wrapped its claws around her neck and squeezed—

David slammed into the creature so hard that he sent them all tumbling on the ground. The Kara creature let go of Jenny. Without missing a beat, David was on his feet and had slipped behind the creature and held his soul blade to its neck.

"Stop! Stop this!" he hissed. "Snap out of it!"

The creature reeked of rot. Kara's sweet lavender scent was gone. He needed that girl back. He needed his Kara.

"Just come back to me, Kara. Don't make me hurt you. Souls, I don't want to hurt you. Please stop this and come back."

The Kara creature stiffened in his hold, aware of the blade at its throat.

The archfiend watched with a satisfied smile on its creepy perfect face.

David glanced around for Metatron, but his body was gone.

"Fight it," urged David. His hand shook violently. "Fight it, please. Don't make me do it, don't make me—"

The creature slammed the back of her head into David's face. He staggered backward and let her go.

The creature whirled around and hit him with its wing, sending him sprawling to the ground. But he was up on his feet quickly.

Death lunged at him, but he kicked the back of the creature's knees and it stumbled. It turned to face him again.

"Don't do this," said David.

Kara was much stronger than he was.

He waved his soul blade. "Kara, fight it," he said more urgently. "I know you're in there somewhere. This isn't you. Fight it."

But the yellow eyes that watched him showed no hint that Kara was in there. There was only a monster. He could see the hunger in its eyes. He could see the pleasure it took in killing. It was going to eat his angel flesh and devour his soul.

The creature licked its dry gray lips and showed off its teeth as it snarled.

"It's *me*! It's me, David."

But the creature didn't recognize him. He didn't know how to stop this fight without one of them getting killed.

The creature flicked its wrists, and a beam of shadow shot toward him.

David tried to twist out of the way, but he wasn't fast enough.

He saw black and crashed head first into the jagged rock. His body jerked as white-hot pain shot through his limbs, and then his body was limp and unresponsive.

He heard footsteps. He heard Jenny calling his name.

He knew the creature was coming back to finish him off. He was drained. But he tried to gather what strength he had left, not for him, but for Kara. He had to try to make the creature remember. She had to remember who she was before the transformation. He would try to make her remember, even if it meant dying in the process.

Something hard hit him in the stomach, and he went sprawling, rolling on the ground.

Why wasn't it killing him yet?

As he lay with his back on the ground, he realized it wanted to play with him.

A tingling in his fingers. Then his toes. He could feel his arms tingling, and although his limbs burned, he winced and willed himself to move. He rolled over and pushed himself up back on his feet.

He saw that Jenny was on her knees with two higher demons holding her. One of them held a death blade to her neck. Her green eyes were dim, like she'd given up.

The Kara creature grinned, and David could tell it was glad he wasn't dead yet. It wanted to keep fighting. It eyed the soul blade he still clasped in his hands.

David couldn't see Kara anywhere inside the monster she had become.

It stepped forward.

"Remember the first time we kissed?" he blurted.

It was a long shot, but he was desperate.

The creature halted, a frown materialized on its face. Was it remembering?

"We were out together at that club, and you kissed me," he said.

He felt a gush of hope and energy.

"Or was it that *I* kissed you first." He shook his head. "Doesn't matter. But you remember, don't you? How it felt? How we both felt?"

The creature stared at him for a long moment, and David was positive that somewhere in there it was remembering.

Kara was still in there, and she was going to wake…

"Kill him," roared the archfiend suddenly. Although her face was twisted in rage, David detected a little fear in her voice as well.

"I command you. Kill this miserable angel speck. We have lots more to kill. Devour this wretched angel soul. Do it. Do it now!"

The Kara creature watched its master then slowly turned its yellow eyes back on David. But it hesitated. It was unsure.

"You know me, don't you?" David's eyes flashed with hope. "Kara, I lo—"

"KILL HIM!"

The creature flicked its wrists. A beam of shadow slammed into David, and he fell back. But he regained his footing, surprised that she hadn't hit him that hard. He made to grab the creature as it dove for him, but it ducked and dodged not letting him get a hold.

It lunged at him again, and David ducked and hit the creature in the head with the pommel of his blade. The creature gagged, dropped back a little, and shook its head. Its eyes looked disconnected and stunned. It stood there for a moment…

David glanced at his blade. He could do it. He could finish her with one stroke—

But he couldn't. He watched her and knew he couldn't hurt her.

The creature watched him curiously and then roared in anger. It dove at him, fangs bared and mouth snapping toward his neck.

His blade was heavy in his hands, but still he couldn't bring himself to use it on her. He couldn't.

He fell against the creature. It tried to bite him, but he jumped away and kicked it hard.

"Enough of this," bellowed the archfiend. "Kill him now, or I will!"

Darkness pulsed through the Kara creature's veins. It boiled inside her and then leaped from her hands in a twisting stream that coursed the distance between them and washed over David.

It happened so quickly that he was unable to escape the flow of dark shadows that shot out through her fingers like bullets.

David wasn't aware that the creature loomed over him. He was barely aware of anything except for the pain.

A wild grin spread on the creature's lips. Its yellow eyes blinked at him, and it picked him up in its strong arms.

David felt his life force seep out of him. The darkness grabbed hold of his soul. It wouldn't be long now. He felt his own death approaching.

He was barely aware that his blade still hung in his hand. He could just reach out, slice the creature's neck, and end it.

But he couldn't. He wouldn't.

Even though she was killing him, this monster was the closest thing he had to Kara.

His Kara...

His blade fell from his fingers. He closed his eyes and let the darkness come.

CHAPTER 23
AWAKENING

Death held the angel in its grasp, squeezing the life force out of it, feeding off of it. It enjoyed killing, especially an angel. It quivered in delight just at the thought of its delicious soul, the sweetness of it. But it didn't want to kill it right away. Not yet. First, it would play with it. Death loved to see the fear in the eyes of its prey before it reached in and took away its soul.

Death knew its master was angry with it for not killing the angel right away, but it was curious about the angel. It didn't understand why, but it felt drawn to this particular angel. It wanted to know why. Why this one? Why was it interested in this angel?

Death decided it would keep him alive for just a little while longer.

"Kill it, you insolent creature!" cried the female archfiend. "I command it. Obey me at once, you vile creature. I am your master now, and you will do what I say. Do your duty and kill the angel."

Death eyed its master. It didn't like to be ordered around. It was strong, very strong. It knew its masters were still weak. It knew that the masters were all waiting for the last seal to be broken. Soon.

But for now, it grew angry. It wanted its master to stop telling it what to do. Death was no one's pet. Death was its own being, the strongest of the four knights, perhaps even stronger than the masters.

It smiled wickedly at the thought. Yes. It was powerful.

As it held the male angel still, it thought about the other three knights. It sensed they were near, waiting in the shadows for the final seal to break. They were all waiting for her to unleash her power, to break the final seal and kill all the angels.

But right now Death didn't care. It only wanted to play with the curious little angel again.

What had it called it before?

The angel had called it Kara, a human name. Strange. Why had that name meant something?

A small light glowed in the depths of Death's being.

"I swear to you by the Darkness that if you don't kill this angel speck now and obey me, I will destroy you!" yelled its master in a fury.

As Death stared into the archfiend's angry face, the light in the pit of its core flickered again and grew.

Death tossed the angel to the ground.

What was happening?

It ignored the strange light it felt inside and focused its cruelty on the angel. The master wanted it dead, but Death was going to play with the young angel before she took its life.

The angel blinked and opened its eyes.

Death waited. It wanted the angel to stand and fight back. It wanted a stronger opponent. It was more fun with a stronger prey for the chase.

The angel cried and tried to scramble to his feet, but Death was faster. She grabbed the angel and sent him crashing to the stone floor again.

Another flicker of light danced inside Death's chest.

Death smiled wickedly, licked its gray lips, and seized the boy by his neck. It raised him high in the air, enjoying the fear in his eyes. It relished the fear. The angel struggled, but it was no use. Death was upon him.

"Kara, please, don't," choked the angel.

What was it about this angel?

Death was hungry to taste this angel's life force. Her black tendrils crept over the angel's body until they covered his face like a spider's web. She was draining his soul. It was a good and pure life force, and Death enjoyed it.

"I—love—you," breathed the angel.

The angel's lips trembled, "I—forgive—you."

The angel looked at Death straight in the face and smiled. And then his eyes rolled back into his head.

The angel's limp body was in Death's grip, and she leaned in to devour his soul. She opened her mouth, longing to taste its purity and power—

But then it recoiled.

Something wasn't right.

Death had sensed it before, but what was it? Why would this miserable angel forgive her for devouring his soul? Was this a trick?

The angel was unconscious and close to death. Death had already eaten bits of his essence.

Why did that smile mean something?

The warm light pulsed inside Death with more urgency now. She staggered and stepped away from the angel. Confused, Death stared at her hands. She didn't know why she had let it go.

"What are you doing, Death?" roared the archfiend. "Kill it. I command you to finish him off. Kill the angel now!"

But Death just stood there, staring at the young angel's face. There was something about his face…

Death knew that face. The face meant something to her.

"Kill it now! Take the soul! I am your god. You will obey, or I will destroy you faster than I created you." The archfiend was furious.

But Death felt compelled to look at the pained face of the young angel.

The light in her intensified. The cold pit in Death's soul began to warm.

White light and pain shot through Death's head. She couldn't move or think. The darkness fought with the light inside her.

The golden, warm pulsing light was winning.

Images and memories, sensations and emotions were all mixing up, matching up, latching on to each other, and splitting off from each other inside her. The darkness struggled with the invasive warm light. The light inside Death was looking for something, searching for someone…

Warm light suddenly pulsed through Death and shone into her cold darkness. She stared at her illuminated body. The red veins retreated from her skin and disappeared. Her body throbbed with a hot, golden energy that must always have always been inside her. And now it was unleashed.

The wild, golden light warmed the darkness inside her, until nothing remained of the cold, damp, dark power.

Kara stared at the golden power that danced around her palms. She spread her brilliant, pulsing, golden butterfly wings, looked up at the archfiend and smiled.

"I'm back."

CHAPTER 24
ELEMENTAL

Kara did two things immediately.

She rushed over to David to make sure he was still alive, and at the same time, she shot two beams of golden light into the two higher demons that held Jenny. They burst into clouds of dust.

Golden sparks of wild energy danced around her body. Her skin shone like it had been painted with liquid gold. She radiated power, elemental power, and she felt stronger than she'd ever felt before.

Kara turned to face the archfiend. She raised her hands, and her elemental power glowed with fierce energy.

"Impossible." The archfiend female staggered back, confused.

"It's not possible. Simply *not* possible. You are the fourth knight! You have the darkness in your essence. It cannot be defeated. We studied for thousands of years to make your ingredients perfect—to put the exact amount, the exact percentage—to make your change irreversible. How can this be?"

Kara moved slowly, her anger boiling inside her and ready to pop.

"Guess your calculations were wrong, *speck*."

She glared at the real monster, the monster that had tried to change her into a beast. She suffered from the guilt she felt about what she had done as Death. She could never undo what she'd done, and that would haunt her forever.

But she could make things right again.

She remembered the white oracle's prophecy.

The only way to stop the archfiends is with the demise of the knight.

Kara *was* that knight. She realized that she was the one that had needed to die. The oracle's prophecy seemed to have been correct.

And now she only needed to nudge it along.

She looked the archfiend in the face.

"You're going to pay for this and for the lives of all the angels you took. You don't belong in this world, and you never have. You don't respect it. You don't love it, and you don't deserve it. You deserve to be sent back to your cage."

The archfiend's face twisted in rage.

"Never. Never will I set foot in that…that dungeon."

The archfiend laughed.

"What? You think you can cage us up again? You? A little angel speck? Don't be foolish. Even the best of your kind weren't able to vanquish us. What makes you so sure that you can do it?"

It was Kara's turn to smile. "I'll figure out a way. Trust me."

Kara felt the golden ring on her finger and rolled it gently. She could feel the reverberations in the energy fields that surrounded the Earth.

She also could sense the thousands of demons that were slowly making their way toward her.

The archfiend saw Kara's shoulders tense.

"There is still time to fix this little...hiccup."

Black mist coiled around the archfiend's hands and fingers.

"We will not go back. I will not go back. I will find a way to change you back, to put you right again."

"I'm perfectly fine the way I am, thank you."

Kara felt a shift in the air, and even before she saw them, she knew that all the other archfiends were coming. She looked to the sky. The dark web had vanished. All the creatures of the Netherworld stopped to watch as the other five archfiends landed next to the female.

The faces of all the archfiends were disturbingly beautiful. But it was a cold and intense beauty. She sensed the evil in that beauty now. They stared at Kara, and she could see the wild fury in their cat-like eyes. Oh boy, were they angry with her.

She gave them her best smile, a smile that David would be proud of.

She watched as Jenny knelt beside David and was surprised and relieved when he sat up. The color had returned to his dazzling blue eyes.

He smiled at her, and she felt a pang in her chest. She had almost killed him. Well, Death had. She couldn't think about that now.

The air moved around her, and Beelzebub landed in front of Kara with a flap of his great wings.

He inspected her slowly, and then his voice boomed, "Tilia! What is the meaning of this? Where is Death?"

The female archfiend held her head high. "I'm...I'm not sure. The creature just slipped away, vanished, and left this one instead. I can't explain it. Perhaps there was a mistake with the extract—"

"There was no mistake," growled Beelzebub. "Not in the extract."

He turned to Kara. "She did this. Somehow, she destroyed the essence, our essence."

"What of the seals?" asked one of the male archfiends? "Has the final seal broken?"

"It hasn't," interrupted Kara. All the archfiends turned their attention on her. "It's not broken. You failed. And now it's only a matter of time before you return to your cages forever."

"I will destroy you!" Tilia flicked her wrists and beams of shadow shot straight for Kara.

But Kara was ready, and in a flash of golden light, she darted out of the way. The shadows merely scorched the ground where Kara had been.

Kara grinned as she looked into Tilia's surprised face.

But then Tilia's surprised look turned into a grin of her own, and she unleashed her fury again, but this time at David.

But Kara was already moving. She shot into the air faster than she'd ever moved before and gathered David and Jenny into her arms. She protected them with her body as the beams of darkness hit.

Although Kara yelled in pain as the darkness coiled around her, and the feeling of death tried to enter her again, she did not succumb to it. Her elemental power broke free of the tendrils of darkness and blasted them into tiny particles.

Kara turned from her friends very slowly. She was trembling with uncontrollable anger. She was going to rip them to shreds.

But then she saw something in their eyes, something that told her that she needn't worry.

She could see fear in Beelzebub's perfect face.

Kara knew that he sensed the change. He sensed that his time left on Earth was short.

The archfiends began to shimmer. Their bodies were fading away like ghosts.

Kara knew what she needed to do. Her elemental power blazed around her like a glowing star. Let them all tremble in fear of the monster that they had woken. Kara soared into the sky in a blaze of golden light.

She spotted the three knights hiding nearby and saw their recognition of her power in their eyes as she neared them. They brandished their weapons and pressed their steeds toward her. But it didn't matter. She was light, and they were darkness. They didn't belong.

She screamed her rage, for all the mortals they had killed. "Murderers!"

Kara became a whirlwind of black shadows and wings. She cut through the knights as though they were mere paper cutouts. With a last flicker, their bodies turned into dust, and the knights shimmered and disappeared.

Suddenly the ground shook below her feet, and she could hear screaming. But it wasn't angels crying for help, this was something else.

Kara glided back to David and Jenny. She could see it had already begun.

A beam of fire erupted from the bowels of the earth, shot up through the air, and tore a hole in the sky. It was just like the rift she had seen before. It wavered and shimmered. It looked as if it were waiting for something.

Then the archfiends cried out. Their bodies wavered and started to fall apart. An invisible force was pulling at them. One by one the archfiends were sucked into the portal and disappeared.

Beelzebub grabbed on to a large boulder and yelled at Kara. "I will return! I will destroy you! I will destroy you all!"

But suddenly his body disintegrated, and he was swallowed up by the portal, just like the others.

The archfiends had been beaten.

Cheers rose up, and Kara turned to see the smiling faces of the angels that had stayed behind and survived.

With grim determination, the angels unleashed their fury on the demons.

It wasn't like anything she'd ever seen. They fought with purpose and ferocity. They fought like they were going to win.

A battle cry sounded, and Kara saw Metatron charge into combat, slicing and dicing his way through the hordes of demons.

"Kara! Kara! Kara!" The angels shouted her name as a battle cry. Now they had something to fight for.

Without their endless supply of power, the demons retreated and vanished into the cliffs and back into the dark depths of the volcano, back to their Netherworld.

The angels had won the war.

CHAPTER 25

A NEW DAWN

The cheering lasted all through the night after the last of the demons had disappeared. The angels celebrated their victory. The mortal world and Horizon were safe.

Although her M-suit was on its last legs, Kara stayed behind. She didn't want to go back to Horizon. Not just yet.

She stood on the spot where she'd last seen the archfiends. The angry gray clouds slowly dissipated to reveal a night sky that glimmered with stars. Memories of what she'd done in the name of Death pulled at her heart. These were things that she'd have to live with. There was no other choice.

The thought of losing Mr. Patterson pained her the most.

"What are you thinking about?" David moved next to her.

Kara gave him a slow, bitter smile. "I can't believe I nearly killed you."

"Nah, you didn't. Not even close," he teased. "I was just pretending. I was doing the gentleman thing and making you think you were winning, when in fact you weren't."

Kara's laugh died in her throat. She looked as if she were overwhelmed with sadness.

"Tell me. What's the matter? What's in that head of yours that's putting on such a sad face?"

With a trembling voice, Kara recounted the events that had led to the oracle's death.

"It wasn't your fault," David said gently. She couldn't look him in the eye.

"You can't blame yourself for this. He wouldn't want you to."

That part was true. Kara knew that Mr. Patterson wouldn't have wanted her to feel guilty about his death. He had chosen to come with her, even though she had asked him not to.

Kara looked up into David's eyes.

"Are oracles like angels? Will his soul live on?"

"I'm not sure, but something tells me that they do. He's probably back in Horizon waiting for you."

"I hope you're right." Kara smiled briefly. "Most of this was my fault you know, whether you want to admit it or not. They used me to do horrible things—"

"That you had no control over." David grabbed her shoulders and made her face him.

"It wasn't you. The Kara I know would never hurt anyone. I know you're stubborn, and most of the time you think you're

269

right—and you are sometimes—but not with this. What the archfiends did was not your fault."

Even though she knew David was right, it would take her a long time to come to terms with what she'd done. David couldn't possibly understand. But she loved him for trying to keep her spirits up.

David…

She'd almost killed him, and yet here he was, full of admiration and with love sparkling in his eyes. She trembled with the temptation to pull him into her and kiss him.

"Here she is," said a familiar voice.

Kara's spirit rose at the sight of Jenny, Peter and Ashley.

"Thank the souls, you're all safe."

Kara's troubles washed away momentarily as she took in the sight of her friends, alive and well. She threw her arms around them and squeezed them in a hug, ignoring Peter's protests and pulling him in, too.

Finally she let them go. "I'm so glad to see you guys. You have no idea. I couldn't bear the thought of losing any of you. You're all so very special to me."

"You're special to us too, Kara," said Peter, but he avoided her eyes.

"Well, you'll be surprised to know that a lot more of us did survive." Ashley gave a wave of her sword. It was still caked with dried demon blood.

"There were casualties, of course, but more injuries than deaths. It's a miracle I think."

"I don't know much about miracles, but it's a relief to see you safe." Kara's chest swelled as she watched their happy faces.

"We all saw what you did, Kara." Peter straightened his shattered glasses on his nose, and Kara wondered why he even bothered to wear them. "You saved us. You did it."

"We all did," said Kara, a little embarrassed. "This is everyone's victory. We all played an important part in it."

"Maybe," said David. "But you most of all." He caught her eye, and she couldn't look away.

"Well, I told you she was a fairy." Jenny's eyes brightened at the sight of Kara's wings. "A golden fairy."

Everyone burst out laughing, including Kara. Her friends' laughter was the most beautiful thing she'd ever heard. She never wanted it to end.

"Truthfully, I don't know how long I'll have them." Kara had already sensed that her golden wings, like weights, were gradually lifting from her shoulders.

"I can't explain it, but I feel like they're leaving me. Like I won't have them for much longer."

"Well, that's too bad because we could have used them." The archangel Ariel walked slowly toward them. Her metal armor was stained with black blood, and her grin was fierce.

"You never cease to amaze me, Kara." Ariel beamed. "The legion is lucky to have you. But something tells me you're not as thrilled as the rest of us."

"I did some terrible things when I was Death."

Ariel put a hand on her shoulder. "You just said it, as Death, not as Kara. That wasn't you. And we can't hold you accountable for something that horrible creature did."

"Told you," whispered David.

"Ariel's right." Metatron's cigar dangled from his lips.

Immediately Kara knew there was something different about him. His entourage was missing. *Were they dead?* She didn't like the lipstick angels, but she didn't necessarily want them dead. Well, not all of them.

"You were possessed. You were being controlled by a demon," continued the big archangel. "You were not yourself, and the legion doesn't condemn angels who have been possessed. Under our laws, an angel who is not in control of their actions cannot be convicted of any crime."

"Am I still under arrest, though?"

Kara had the feeling that even though they had won the war, Metatron didn't forgive or forget easily. "For the other thing?"

Metatron looked at Kara with a blank face.

"In view of recent events, let's just say the arrest warrant has been lifted." He exhaled a cloud of gray smoke. "For now, that is."

Kara shot David a look and tried to control the laugh that wanted to burst from her mouth.

But then she lost her smile and turned to Ariel.

"What about the mortal world? All the diseases and the lands poisoned by the knights? All those sick people? What's going to happen to them?"

"The mortal world will heal. The crops will grow back. The animals will thrive again, and the sick will recover. It has already begun. Most mortals will not remember this experience, the oracles are already back hard at work adjusting memories and correcting lapses in time."

"And the archfiends?" Kara's eyes moved to Metatron, but he only seemed interested in his cigar.

"They used up all of their resources," answered Ariel. "They cannot break free. I can say it with confidence. They will never break out again."

Kara couldn't help but feel a little proud at what she had helped accomplish. The world was safe, for now, and now was certainly good enough.

Ariel put her hand back on Kara's shoulder.

"I came here to thank you on behalf of my fellow archangels and of the entire legion. I also wanted to tell you something, Kara."

"What thing?"

"You'll be happy to know that you've been given a special leave from the legion."

Kara wrinkled her brow. "Like a *permanent* leave?"

It was too good to be true, a dream come true.

"In a matter of speaking, yes." Ariel smiled. "I know it's something you've wanted for a long time, and no one deserves it more than you, Kara Nightingale. I believe the fate of the mortal world and Horizon will be safe from any enemies for a *very* long time."

Kara's eyes brightened. "I—I don't know what to say?"

"*Thank you* would be a start," laughed David smugly.

She'd have punched him if she didn't want to kiss him so much.

"Thank you."

Kara was aware that masses of guardians had gathered around and were listening to their conversion and trying to get a closer look at her. She could tell by their timid expressions that they didn't want to push in, but that they still wanted to watch.

"You'll be missed," said Ariel. "By everyone. That's a promise."

"But mostly by me." David's eyes shone the deepest blue. It was the most beautiful thing she'd ever seen.

And then she did something that she never thought she'd be able to do. Even though Metatron, Ariel, and all the other guardians were watching her, she cupped David's face in her hands and kissed him.

She kissed him softly at first, but then she kissed him fiercely. She crushed her lips on his, like there was no one else in the world but her and him. She kissed him again and again. Then she grabbed the back of his hair and pulled him into her so she could drink in his wonderful scent.

David wrapped his arms around her tightly and kissed her back. Her elemental energy pulsed. Angels' touches and kisses were a thousand times more electrifying than mortal ones. She never wanted it to end.

Finally she pulled back, suddenly aware that many eyes were watching. But the smile on David's face, the love that danced in his eyes, was worth it.

Ariel smiled at her brightly. Even Metatron had a goofy look on his face as he puffed on his cigar.

Applause filled the air. Guardians whistled and cheered. Ashley and Jenny laughed and clapped their hands. Even Peter, who stood with his hands in his pockets, wore the widest grin she'd ever seen.

David's eyes were wide. "I can't believe you did that. In front of everyone! Don't get me wrong, you've made me really, really happy, and I really, really liked it but...you sure you're all right?"

"I'm more than all right." Kara didn't fight her own grin. "I haven't felt this good, this amazing, in a very long time."

She squeezed David's hand. "Let's go home."

CHAPTER 26

HOME

"**So** they're saying it was a tornado?" Kara had been drilling the old man with questions for the past hour.

"But we don't get tornadoes here. We get snow storms."

Mr. Patterson polished the surface of his brand-new counter.

"I'll admit it does sound preposterous, especially here, but on rare occasions this city has seen one or two tornadoes."

Kara screwed up her face. "I don't know. It doesn't make sense."

"Are you a weather specialist? An atmospheric scientist? A tornado expert?"

"No…but then how come Cedarview didn't get hit? It's the next street over? They're saying it was a big one, so why *only* our street? If it really was a tornado, why did it skip all the other streets in the entire city and just plow into ours? It's almost like something was *controlling* it. You know what I mean?"

The old man shrugged.

"No. But Mother Nature is mysterious in her ways. Can you hand me that small red box over there, the one with tiny crystal orbs? Yes, that one. Careful please, I've only just replaced them. Thank you."

Kara watched Mr. Patterson as he carefully emptied the box of crystals and placed them into his glass display counter. She would never truly understand his fascination with glass orbs.

The last streaks of sun spilled in through the front bay window.

"Are you happy the shop's almost back to its pre-tornado state? If you truly believe that's what happened."

He was still gazing adoringly at the crystal orbs.

"There's still a little painting to be done on the exterior walls and the front sign, but it's almost done."

The old man let out a long sigh. "Yes. It's been a rather a *complicated* week."

"What do you mean complicated?"

Kara hated how her boss continued to speak in riddles. She always had the feeling that he was keeping information from her, like he didn't trust her.

No, she was just being foolish. What secrets could an old bookstore owner truly have?

"It's not important anymore," replied Mr. Patterson. "What's important is that our lives are back to what they were before the apocalypse—"

The old man dropped one of his precious crystals.

"The apocalypse?" Kara leaned over the counter, snatched up the rolling orb, and held it up to inspect it. "If that's what you want to call it. But I don't see how the damage to our street can be called an apocalypse."

Mr. Patterson looked irritated.

"Never mind that. I'll take that back now."

Kara lowered the crystal but still didn't give it back. Not yet.

"I'd like to know your thoughts, on this *apocalypse*, as you call it."

She couldn't explain it, but she had the strangest feeling that Mr. Patterson didn't think it had been a tornado after all. He kept avoiding her eyes when she mentioned it, like he wasn't able to lie. What could have been aimed at their street and destroyed it like a bomb had gone off? What was he keeping her from her?

"What happened to the rest of the world, then?"

She handled the orb between her fingers. "What's your theory on that?" she asked. "I'll admit a lot of strange things have happened lately. Don't you think this past week's been really odd?"

"Not more than usual, dear." Mr. Patterson eyed the crystal in Kara's hand.

"What? Where have you been?"

The old man held out his hand. "I'll take that now, thank you."

Feeling a little rebellious, Kara tossed the crystal orb in the air, but the old man caught it before she had time to blink.

She pulled back, shocked and impressed.

"Okay, it's not like I was going to keep it or anything. So..."

She leaned over the counter.

"For the past week, there have been reports of strange occurrences all around the world. Crops dried out, but then miraculously grew back the next day. Sick animals and people were suddenly cured of incurable diseases. And there's peace in the world, well, for the most part. Most people on the Internet are calling it an environmental disaster or an example of global warming. But the truth is, I haven't found any *real* evidence to explain what happened last week. No scientist can explain it. Don't you think that's strange?"

"Stranger things have happened."

Kara rolled her eyes.

"Fine. Be in one of those *mysterious* moods."

The sound of construction outside spilled in through the window.

"Well, it's five o'clock. I'm done for the day."

She brushed the dust from the front of her shirt and inspected her jeans to make sure they were spotless.

"I'm off with David to catch dinner and movie."

The thought of spending two hours with David sent a nervous flutter through her chest. This wasn't their first date, yet she felt overly nervous. Her heart pounded in her ears. Why was she being so silly?

"Bye, Mr. P."

As she turned to leave, she paused when she caught the delight in Mr. Patterson's eyes. "What? What's that face for?"

Mr. Patterson's smiled. "Nothing, dear. Just glad you're out and about, having fun just like you should be."

And then he added in a whisper, but not low enough. "After all, no one deserves it more than you."

Kara's brows narrowed slightly.

"Huh? Well, thanks I guess. But I haven't done more than usual, maybe a little painting."

She watched him for a moment, but his expression didn't change.

"Okay then, thanks." Her smile returned. "There aren't many warm nights like this left."

"Yes," said the old man, still watching her with that bemused expression. "I believe you are right."

"See you tomorrow," Kara pushed open the front door of the tiny bookstore and jumped onto the street.

A breeze cooled her hot cheeks. The evening sky was still a bright blue, and although the days were getting shorter, it was a perfect evening for a date.

A handsome young man leaned against a parked car. He wore jeans and a simple white t-shirt that clung to his body, just enough to hint at the muscles beneath. The evening sun kissed his tanned features, and his skin glowed.

Kara's heart caught in her throat.

"You look nice," said David, causally. "Better than nice."

Heat rushed to her face, and she failed to keep a giant smile from spreading over her face.

"So, where are you taking me?" she asked.

"It's a surprise."

He smiled at her, and she felt her knees go weak.

As she and David began to walk along the sidewalk, something in the reflection on the store's bay window caught her attention. She halted.

"What?" said David. "Did you forget to clean a spot on the window?"

Kara frowned and touched the glass. "No. That's not it. I thought...I thought for a moment..."

David leaned closer, his arm touching hers. "You thought what?"

Kara swallowed hard. Bracing herself, she said, "It's going to sound really weird, but for a moment I thought I saw wings."

"Wings?" laughed David playfully.

"Golden wings," she said with a straight face. "Glorious wings. They were shining like something out of a fairy tale. You think I'm crazy, don't you? And now you're wondering what you're doing with such a nut case."

David twirled a lock of her hair in his fingers.

"Yes. You're nuts. But that's what I love about you. You keep it interesting."

Kara was about to object, but he put his hands on her waist and pulled her closer to him. He leaned in and kissed her.

The kiss was like coming home or being born again. They had kissed before, but somehow this was different, more intense. His lips were hot and soft against hers, and she trembled at his touch.

She threw her arms around his neck, forgot all about the mysterious golden wings, and embraced the love of her life.

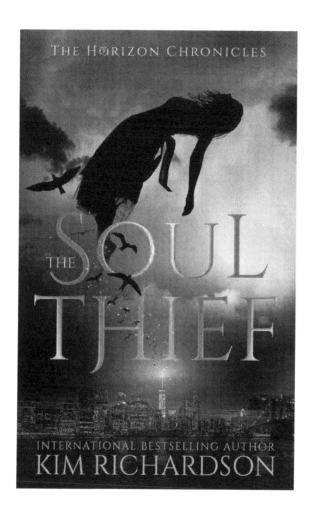

CHAPTER 1

ALEXA KNEW SHE WAS DEAD when she saw the bright light.

It was just like those near-death experiences she'd read about: the tunnel, the white light, the feeling of peace. She felt her physical body detach like the shedding of skin. Floating in total serenity, secure and warm, she soared towards the overwhelming light. She was drawn up into a beam of sunlight like a speck of dust.

The air was cool and thick, humid and salty, like a sea breeze. The pain of the accident had melted away, and the light welcomed her.

Deep down, Alexa knew she should be afraid. She should be terrified. But for the first time in her life she wasn't afraid.

She saw a pinpoint of dark shadow in the distance. As she drifted towards it, she could see it was the entrance to a tunnel. No. Not a tunnel, but an elevator. Suddenly she was riding in an elevator.

She did not speak to the ape-like creature that operated the elevator. She spread her arms and looked down at her hands. She could see the floor through her hands. She wasn't solid.

Still, she wasn't afraid.

The elevator rocked, and the doors slid open. As she stepped out, the creature muttered something that sounded a lot like, *Orientation, level one.*

She knew that animals couldn't speak. She wouldn't have been surprised if she were delusional. It would have been totally acceptable under the circumstances. She was dead.

Maybe her brain didn't function the same way anymore. Maybe nothing did.

The elevator seemed to have disappeared, and Alexa stood in an infinitely long white corridor. She could hear thousands of voices murmuring, and she began to feel anxious.

Alexa had never seen so many people all at once. It looked as if every ethnic group from the human race was milling around busily in a maze of offices and corridors. And for the first time since she'd died, she felt frightened again.

She tried to hide the terror that shook her as she followed the crowds.

Within a few minutes she arrived at an ancient building with a mammoth oak door. A neon sign zapped and crackled above it.

Oracle Division # 998-4589. Orientation.

Orientation. It was the same word she thought she'd heard on the elevator. Perhaps the creature had spoken. Where was she?

Alexa wished she were back in the elevator with the light and that feeling of protective warmth. She had felt safe there. Dread gripped her now.

She braced herself, pulled open the door, and stepped inside.

She stood in a large library-like room with corridors and passageways that led to smaller offices. Books and filing cabinets were stacked precariously all the way to the ceiling. The air was thick with the same salty ocean fragrance she had smelled earlier, and she could hear what sounded like pebbles rolling on a smooth marble floor.

A door touched her behind as it opened, and she froze.

Huge glass spheres with tiny bare-foot old men balancing on top of them like circus acrobats rolled into the library. The tiny men wore silver gowns, and their long white beards flowed behind them as they maneuvered the balls between the piles of books and files. It was the most incredible sight.

She was transfixed.

They were so preoccupied with their work that they didn't appear to notice her at all. If she wasn't important to them, she knew wherever she was couldn't be so bad. It certainly wasn't as bad as dying.

Alexa could see what appeared to be another smaller office to her right. Cabinets were stacked on top of each other in there as well, and what looked like a five-foot round pool was mounted in the back corner. Another one of those tiny men sat on a large crystal ball behind a semi-circular wooden desk.

"Come in, come in, Alexa Dawson," he said in a strange, high-pitched voice, a voice that sounded like he had inhaled helium from a balloon.

Alexa tried to ignore the creepy fact that this stranger knew her name. But her apprehension faded as soon as she saw the man's cheerful face. Still, she approached him carefully, and as she did she noticed a soft, silver light radiating all around him.

Finally, she found her voice. "Is this—" She cleared her throat and felt relieved that her voice sounded the same. It was *her* voice. "Is this heaven?"

Back in life, she had never given any real thought to heaven, or even the possibility of an afterlife. She had just never imagined she'd be dead at seventeen.

The man's face lit up, and his blue eyes sparkled. "Horizon has many names. Heaven is one, yes, just like Utopia, or Shangri-La, or Zion. Ultimately, it doesn't matter what name you choose. They all mean the same thing. It's where everything originated, and the place to which mortals return in the afterlife."

"The afterlife," repeated Alexa, testing the words on her mouth. "I'm dead. Truly dead."

"Yes."

"I knew it, you know, that I *was* dead. It's just strange to hear it. To say it out loud." Alexa reached up and touched her face, her neck, checking to make sure she was there. Her face was just as solid as the rest of her. But there was something missing. And when it came to her, she thought she must have been stupid not to have noticed before.

The rhythmic beating in her chest that had accompanied her throughout her life was silent. She had no heart.

When she looked up, she found the man's eyes showed his concern for her.

"You'll be fine," he said. His gentle tone was strangely comforting. "Mind you, it takes a bit of adjusting in the beginning. But sooner or later, every soul adjusts, and you'll be as right as rain in no time. I promise you."

Alexa focused on his smiling face and did her best to keep her fears from showing. She would keep her cool. She would not freak out. Not yet.

The tiny man clapped his hands together. "A mortal death is never the end...just the beginning of something more exciting." He spoke as if her mortal death was the best news ever, a great revelation.

While Alexa's anxiety subsided a bit, her curiosity increased. She couldn't help it. It was her nature to want to know about things, especially when they concerned the great mysteries of life.

"Are you an angel?"

The man chuckled at that. "Yes and no. I'll keep it simple for you. I'm an oracle. Archangels, guardian angels, oracles, and other ethereal beings dwell here in Horizon. It is home and headquarters for the immortals who govern and protect the mortal world from evil."

While this revelation should have energized her, Alexa mourned the loss of her mortal life. All the what-ifs and dreams she'd hoped one day to accomplish had been for nothing. She could see that the oracle sensed her discomfort.

"Tell me, Alexa," he asked her gently, "what's the last thing you remember?"

Images flashed in her mind's eye. "I was at school," replied Alexa. Her mind began to clear, and images began moving and coming together of their own volition, forming solid, real memories. "I remember falling. That's right. I remember now. I was carrying my laptop with a stack of books and must have missed a step… I fell down the stairs, and I heard something snap. Then nothing. And then I woke up here."

The fall had killed her. She'd died at school during lunch. It had been the worst possible time because everyone would have been out of class. Her entire high school would have witnessed her death.

She felt a rush of humiliation pass through her. It was a cold, prickly sensation. *What must she have looked like!* …on the floor, with the entire school looking at her dead body, her neck bent at an unnatural angle. She was horrified.

But her embarrassment was nothing compared to the sadness she now felt.

Her best friend Emma Middletown had moved away last summer, and she had made no other friends. No one would remember her. No one cared that she was dead. Not her deadbeat father, who liked his new family better. Nor her mother, who would probably have been too drunk to notice she was missing.

The fact of the matter was, not a single soul would miss her…

"It'll be all right, Alicia," said the oracle. His high-pitched voice was reassuring, and his whole face beamed.

Alexa opened her mouth to correct his mistake about her name but then thought better of it. She had the unnerving feeling that somehow the oracle had read her mind.

The oracle leaned forward on his desk. "Every single thing that happened in your life was to prepare you for what's to come. Remember that." He raised his hands. "For this."

Alexa shrugged. "But I'm only seventeen. It's not like I've had lots of life experiences. Apart from having had a textbook case of a dysfunctional family, which I have *loads* of experience with, by the way, and which would have made me an excellent guidance counselor, I haven't achieved anything. I'm not even out of my teens, and sometimes I secretly wish I were twelve again. I can't even cook an omelet without burning the eggs." She paused when she realized that she was prattling on. "Prepare me for what exactly?"

The oracle's brilliant teeth shone like stars when he smiled. "Because today, young lady, you'll begin your training as a guardian angel."

About the Author

Kim Richardson is the award-winning author of the bestselling SOUL GUARDIANS series. She lives in the eastern part of Canada with her husband, two dogs and a very old cat. She is the author of the SOUL GUARDIANS series, the MYSTICS series, and the DIVIDED REALMS series. Kim's books are available in print editions, and translations are available in over 7 languages.

To learn more about the author, please visit:

Website
www.kimrichardsonbooks.com
Facebook
https://www.facebook.com/KRAuthorPage
Twitter
https://twitter.com/Kim_Richardson_

88874096R00177

Made in the USA
Middletown, DE
12 September 2018